MURDER IN THE MEDITATION

KARI LEE TOWNSEND

OLIVER
HEBER
BOOKS

GNARLY WOOL PUBLISHING
EST. 2005

0 9 8 7 6 5 4 3 2 1

"There you are, Morty," I said as I scooped up my large, pure white cat with black eyes and carried him into the living room of Divine Inspiration. I snuggled his fluffy head under my chin as I admired the newly renovated inn. My mother's classic taste was a far cry from my laid-back vibe. Morty had always wandered for days at a time, but lately he'd been gone more often and for longer periods. A summer breeze blew in through the open windows, carrying the smell of fresh cut grass and flowers with it, and I could hear the sound of the river out back.

A year and a half ago I had come to Divinity from the Big Apple. The small, upstate New York town was quaint with old-fashioned street lamps and historical buildings. The house I fell in love with was an ancient Victorian house with a massive wraparound porch off of Main Street on Shadow Lane. I'd named her Vicky. I got her for a steal because everyone said she was haunted. Morty had come with the house, and it was apparent from the first night that he was no ordinary cat. He moved at lighting speed, I'd never seen him eat or sleep, and his eyes were so dark. I didn't know *what* he was, so I'd named his Morty—short for immortal.

I never used to worry about him not coming home until now.

"I swear he spends more time here than at home," I said.

"You're married now," my mother, Vivian Meadows, said, looking chic and sophisticated, her golden blond hair artfully styled and tailored black suit more appropriate for a courtroom than to greet her guests. "He knows Mitch will protect you."

My mother had been a tough lawyer and my father a world-renowned cardiologist, but they'd retired and moved to Divinity to be closer to me and to take over Divine Inspiration—the lovely inn on the outskirts of town. They'd had me later in life. I knew they loved me, but two brilliant minds couldn't understand how their only child had chosen to be a fortune teller as a career. They still didn't fully believe in my psychic ability, but they'd finally begun to support my choices, especially since my wedding just two short months ago.

"I'm a grown woman, Mother. I don't need protecting." I stood straighter to make myself look less like the petite Tinkerbell my husband compared me to and more like the capable woman I was. I kissed the top of Morty's soft furry head, and he squirmed as if agitated before leaping from my arms and walking regally out of the room and into the kitchen.

My mother didn't even flinch. She used to be terrified of Morty, but ever since he'd saved her life, she'd softened toward him.

I puckered my forehead. "You don't think he's mad at me for marrying Mitch, do you?" My two favorite fellows had butted heads over the past year and a half, but I'd thought they had come to a truce of sorts after the wedding. They knew I would never choose between them. "Maybe he thinks I abandoned him." I twisted the material of my tie-dyed sundress between my fingers until I saw my mother's raised eyebrow. Letting go, I smoothed the new wrinkles I'd placed there and let out a breath of air.

"Oh, fiddle dee dee, child, that cat knows you love him." Granny Gert waved her wooden spoon in the air then stuck it back in her apron made out of old flour sacks. I'd always been closer to my grandmother than my mother, which didn't sit well with Vivian. Patting her perfectly styled snow-white hair, Granny Gert's snappy brown eyes twinkled. "He's just here to see me." She picked up her pumpkin cookie jar with the foil wrapped plate for a lid. "No one can resist my cookies. Besides, I made him some new summer bowties." Morty didn't like many people, but he'd formed a similar bond with my grandmother as he had with me, even allowing her to dress him up in bowties like my late Grampa Frank.

"My word, everyone knows he likes my famous lemon meringue pie best," Fiona Atwater-Dingleburg said, shaking her salon-bottled, strawberry blond head of hair and batting her contact-enhanced, lavender eyes.

Fiona refused to age. Period. End of story.

She used to be Granny Gert's arch nemesis for decades because she'd had a thing for Grandpa Frank, but he'd chosen my grandmother. Now, after all this time, she married Judge Harry Dingleburg. The Dynamic Duo had made amends for the most part. They were still super competitive, but Great-Grandma Tootsie kept them in line now that they had become the Tasty Trio. They'd come to my mother's rescue in the kitchen as the cooks when she'd needed help with the inn.

"Boys-oh-day, ladies," Great-Grandma Tootsie interrupted, emerging from the kitchen with a plate of breakfast scones that smelled heavenly. Butter and cinnamon had my mouth watering in anticipation of my first bite. "We all know Morty has a mind of his own." She set the tray on the dining room table and turned her faded blue eyes on me. "Sunny, my dear, Morty knows where his home is. He also knows you don't need him as much these days, so he's free to come and go as he pleases." Her face softened as she stared off out the window. "That one's a character, he is. Reminds me of someone I knew a long time ago."

"Your late husband?" I asked, knowing she had been married with children, grandchildren, and great-grandchildren. They had all either passed away or moved, but Toots had decided to return to the town she'd loved most instead of going with them. They had only agreed because staying at the inn was a compromise so she wouldn't be alone. She had amazing skills in the kitchen, so she'd made my mother a deal. Free room and board and she would become her head chef. We all thought that was a crazy idea, given her age.

Until we tasted her cooking.

Now we were all thankful and more than grateful. The woman was a genius in the kitchen and no one could replicate her recipes because she didn't have any. When asked, she would simply say, *Oh, a handful of this and a pinch of that.* My parents planned to throw her a huge surprise birthday party later this year with her family when she would turn one hundred years old.

"Oh, no, dear. My husband was a wonderful man

and we had a good life together, God rest his soul. I'm talking about a man I knew before him." Her faded blue eyes misted. "The love of my life who got away."

"If you don't mind my asking, what happened?" I couldn't imagine finding Mitch and then having to spend a lifetime without him.

"Times were different back then, jobs and money scarce. My father got a job in another state. My mother had passed on, and my father couldn't work and raise my younger siblings alone. So, I sacrificed my own happiness for the sake of my family. I came back to Divinity a few years later, but the man I knew was no longer there. No one had seen or heard from him in over a year, so I left. Everything happens for a reason, I suppose. I just wish I could have seen him one more time."

Granny Gert's brown eyes were full of mischief and twinkles. "It's never too late for wishes to come true. I loved my Frank dearly, but he would want me to go on living. So, I never stop wishing a certain Captain Grady Walker will finally like me for more than my cookies." She winked, then grew serious. "I have a feeling this summer is going to be full of surprises." Her gaze met mine and held.

I blinked.

Great-Grandma Tootsie adjusted her checkered apron over her polyester pants, breaking the odd energy buzzing between my grandmother and myself. "Enough about me," Toots said. "You are simply glowing, Sunny. Married life agrees with you."

Mitch walked through the doorway to the inn at that moment, followed closely by my father and Harry. Both the older men wore rubber wader overalls, bucket hats, and vests with all sorts of fishing paraphernalia sticking out of the many pockets. Harry carried the tacklebox, and my father carried the poles. Harry was older than my father, and on a mission to carry out his bucket list. Ever since my father had retired, he'd been Harry's shadow. Now, apparently, since Mitch was *officially* part of the family, they were trying to recruit him.

"Come on, Son," my father boomed, clapping Mitch on the shoulder. "There hasn't been a murder in months. Surely you can take the day off."

"That's right, Detective," Harry chimed in. "We'll make it worth your while." He grinned, holding up a cooler of trouble.

"Donald," my mother scolded, and he held his hands up then pointed at Harry, to which my mother simply rolled her eyes.

I tried not to giggle over the look of desperation on my husband's face and decided to have pity on him. He had a hard time saying no to my father. "Sorry, Dad, I'm not ready to share my husband just yet." I walked over to Mitch and looped my arm through his. "Remember, you planned to spend the day with me, honey? We'd better get going if we're going to fit in everything we talked about doing today."

"That's right, babe. I could never forget plans with you." Mitch looked at the guys and shrugged. "Sorry, guys. Can't disappoint the wife." He took my hand, and we made a beeline for the door, double-time.

"Newlyweds," we heard one of the men mutter.

"Give him a while," the other one said. "He'll be the one asking *us* to go fishing soon enough."

We closed the door on their chuckles, followed by muffled offended female voices. Things were different since we'd gotten married, that was for sure. Granny Gert's words came back to me, and I frowned, an uneasy feeling settling into my gut.

I'd never liked surprises.

"Good morning, Mrs. Stone," Mitch whispered in my ear the next morning and then kissed my cheek, his musky cologne lingering after he stepped away. True to his word, he'd taken the day off and played hooky with me yesterday, even though our plans hadn't been real. We spent a nice relaxing day doing nothing.

"I don't think I'll ever get tired of hearing that, Mr. Stone." I turned around in our kitchen and faced Mitch, then glanced throughout the room.

The massive kitchen with her well-worn hardwood floors, antique harvest table, and chipped china was my favorite part of the house. The table sat right by the large windows that allowed glorious rays of sunshine to pour in and warm the area, making the room come alive. The décor in this room, like the rest of the house, was older than my great-grandmother's hope chest. So full of charm and history. I loved it all. There was only one thing wrong.

Morty was missing again.

The house seemed so quiet without him. I couldn't shake the feeling that something was going on with him. I sensed things were off, but I hadn't been able to get a read on my mysterious cat. I'd have to try harder so I would know how to help him. Thank goodness for Mitch, or I would be lonely. It was nice having a husband to share my space with now, but that didn't mean I would ever stop missing Morty.

My gaze traced over Mitch. He was so handsome. Tall and muscular with stormy gray eyes, thick dark wavy hair, and a five o'clock shadow that helped hide the jagged scar along his jawline. He was as dark as I was fair, as grumpy as I was sunny, but I wouldn't go through life with anyone else by my side.

"Can you believe it's only been a year and a half since I moved here? It seems like so much longer." I took a sip of my tea.

"Probably because there have been five murders in Divinity since you moved to town." He raised one eyebrow at me and sipped his strong black coffee.

Divinity was a sleepy small town where not much happened. That was one of the reason's Mitch had moved from being a big-city homicide investigator to a small-town detective. Or at least Divinity used to be quiet until I had moved to town from the Big Apple. Trouble seemed to follow me wherever I went for some reason.

I was psychic, but even I hadn't been able to work this one out.

"Come on, Detective Grumpy Pants, you can't blame all of those murders on me. And, hey, maybe that streak is over now that we're married."

"Did your magic wand tell you that?" He smirked.

"Very funny." I poked him in the chest. "I'm not a fairy, Mr. Know-it-all. I'm a fortune teller."

"Same difference."

I gasped. "Not even close. I don't need magic or fortune-telling tools to see that Divinity has been quiet lately, and I'm not complaining." Mitch had finally admitted that things I predicted tended to come true eventually; however, I wouldn't go as far as to say he was a true believer in my abilities.

He grunted. "Yeah, well, things won't be quiet for long with the Psychic Fair coming to town this weekend. Detective Fuller and I are going to have our hands full. The crazies tend to come out of the woodwork around events like that. On top of everything else, it will be a full moon this weekend. Not that I believe strange things happen because of the moon. I think people *make* themselves crazy because they believe it, resulting in the most bizarre things happening during a full moon." He set his mug in the sink. "I wouldn't be surprised if Mayor Cromwell planned to host the Psychic Fair this weekend on purpose. Now, *there's* one big red-headed nutjob if you ask me."

"He's not crazy just because he believes in psychics." The mayor was my biggest fan and had come to me for weekly readings since I'd moved to town. Mitch didn't like him because the mayor was not a fan of Mitch's and insisted the police use me as a consultant because of my psychic abilities. On the other hand, Chief Spencer wasn't a fan of mine, yet he adored Mitch. At least Captain Walker liked both of us. "I for one am thrilled about the Psychic Fair coming to Divinity. It will be nice to be around people like myself if only for a weekend."

I'd always been psychic, but I didn't start my fortune-telling business until I moved to Divinity. I'd only recently learned there was a whole organization for people like me. The Psychic Fair was for members of the organization. I planned to meet my fellow psychics and join the organization so I could take part in future fairs.

I chewed my bottom lip. "You don't think I'll lose my regular customers, do you?"

"Not a chance, Tink. They love you." He kissed me softly on the lips and then tweaked my nose. "But not as much as I do."

He'd called me Tink, short for Tinkerbell, and I'd called him Grumpy Pants from the moment we'd met.

It had sort of stuck and had turned into terms of endearment.

"You want some eggs for breakfast?" He pulled out a frying pan and spatula then headed for the refrigerator.

The thought of breakfast of any kind had my stomach turning over. I breathed in and out through my nose slowly until my stomach settled. "No thanks. I'll just stick with tea. My stomach's a little off. Must be something I ate last night."

He frowned, his hand holding an open carton of eggs. He'd already cracked three. "We ate the same thing, and I feel fine." He set the carton down and picked up my cell phone, thrusting it in my direction. "Call Doc Wilcox right now."

Mitch had always been over protective, especially after his younger sister died years ago. He was terrified to lose anyone else he loved. Now that we were married, he was worse than ever. All the progress he had made in being more comfortable with me being a consultant for the police department vanished faster than my cat.

I took my phone from him and set it on the counter. "It's probably indigestion or some little stomach bug." He opened his mouth to speak, but I covered his lips with my fingertips. "I'm not going to close up shop over a little tummy ache. I have a full day of clients today. If I don't feel better later, I will cancel the rest of the afternoon and go see the doctor. Okay?" I dropped my hand.

"Sure," he said. I could tell that was hard for him, but at least he was trying.

"Thank you." I kissed his cheek then pointed to the sizzling frying pan. "Better flip those eggs before you burn them like I do."

"Roger that." He quickly returned to cooking.

I headed to my Sanctuary which was safer territory for me. Let's just say my skills did *not* lie in the kitchen. Just before I reached my fortune-telling room, I noticed the horseshoe Morty had given Mitch and me at our wedding to wish us good luck. I'd hung it above my Sanctuary door. What was it doing in the hall on the floor? I looked around, but once again didn't see my mischievous cat. I picked the horseshoe up and rehung it, but couldn't shake the feeling....

Mysterious Morty was still trying to tell me something.

2

Three days later, it was the start of the weekend. The Psychic Fair was set up outside since the forecast looked good. It wasn't supposed to rain until late Sunday night after the fireworks display, so the mayor chose to host the event in Mini Central Park instead of the convention center. All the psychics had tents set up around the park grounds, and our resident swans, Fred and Ginger, kept guard over their pond. The park looked more like a mystical village, with new age music filtering through the speakers and the scent of various essential oils and sage permeating the air. People wandered about from tent to tent receiving readings, as well as frequenting food trucks and venders who were selling fair trinkets and t-shirts. Another event that was good for Divinity's economy.

"There you are." My best friend Joanne Burnham-West thrust a mini version of her fiery-tempered, red-headed self into my arms, his fisted hands and kicking feet flailing in every direction. "Here. Take your godson. He misses you."

Jackhammer Jeremiah stopped moving and stared up at me wide-eyed, then his face scrunched up like he was about to wail. I started bouncing him on my hip, which re-activated the flailing hands and feet once more. "I have two godson's you know." I winced, knowing I was going to have several baby sized bruises down my whole side tomorrow.

"Yeah, but if you can handle *this* one, then you can handle anything. Consider it a crash course in motherhood." Jo took a long drink from her water bottle, looking frazzled and sleep deprived, but happy.

Meanwhile, Jeremiah's twin, Calm Collin, was a perfect replica of his dark-haired, gentle-giant father. He lay peacefully asleep on his big daddy's broad shoulder. Cole was so large we'd all dubbed him Sasquatch, and Jo was a statuesque Amazon. Their babies were off the chart already when it came to their size, and my arms began to ache holding my big, squirming, purple-faced bundle.

"Here, let me take him." Mitch took Jeremiah into his arms, and the boy settled instantly. My husband had been uncomfortable around babies in the past, but he'd quickly adapted to his role as godfather far better than I had as godmother.

Mitch wasn't as big as Cole, but he was still a large man, making me a little worried over how big our kids might be. My stomach flipped over the thought of having a baby. I was the one who had decided I wanted a family, and it had taken a lot of convincing to get Mitch on board. Now that he had embraced the idea of fatherhood, I knew he would be wonderful at it. He was already proving that with the twins.

I was the one who had doubts. I was terrified I would be a horrible mother. No matter what I did, the twins were not comfortable with me. Not very reassuring in the least. My only consolation was that we were newlyweds. We had plenty of time before we had to worry about starting a family.

Zoe, a smaller, softer auburn-haired, pale gray-eyed version of Jo, joined us with her new fiancé, Sean O'Malley. Sean was a former ladies' man. None of us had ever thought the blond-haired, blue-eyed outrageous flirt would ever settle down. One look at Zoe and he was a changed man.

"Hey, boss, the wine order is wrong again today," Sean said. "You might want to check with Rich tomorrow to see what happened."

Sean worked for Jo at her bar, Smokey Jo's Tavern, taking on more responsibility since Jo got married and had the twins. Her husband, Cole, helped out when they needed him, but he had his own construction company to operate. The running of the tavern came down to Jo and Sean pretty much, and she was thinking of making him an equal partner.

"Thanks, Sean," Jo responded. "He might even be here tonight. I know the vendors are serving his wine at the fair."

Rich Hastings owned a small Finger Lakes winery. He was friends with Zoe's ex-boyfriend, Mark Silverman, who was a large animal vet here in Divinity. Zoe and Mark broke up on good terms years ago when she moved away. Jo had told me after Zoe had moved back, Mark thought they would pick up the pieces and start over, but that never happened. Sean won Zoe's heart fair and square, and Mark was left disappointed and broken hearted.

Apparently, he'd never gotten over her.

So, when Mark asked Jo for a favor, she didn't have the heart to say no. She told me she had always liked the guy. She agreed to give Rich a try as her wine distributor, but Sean had caught him messing up two orders already, and she had a business to run. I didn't see Rich lasting long if he didn't get his act together.

"I'll be back, lass." Sean's dimples sank deep as he grinned and let go of Zoe's hand.

"How are the wedding plans going?" I asked Zoe as Sean wandered over to the men to catch up.

"Not very well." Her face looked pale.

"I'm sure it will be great. You're a wedding planner." I reached out and rubbed her arm. "A very good one at that."

"Sure, I always know what to do for other people." She shrugged. "But making decisions for myself is so stressful. Sean's no help. He just keeps saying whatever you want is good for me, love."

"It'll be okay," Jo chimed in as she joined us. "Look at what I went through. My wedding almost didn't happen with Cole backing out 'for my own good,' and then look at Sunny with her cold feet. You were the strong one for us both, reassuring us every step of the way until we got our happy endings. Now it's our turn to be there for you."

"Yup, exactly what Jo said." I nodded and shivered over the thought of what had almost happened. "I'm so happy now, and to think I almost called off my wedding because I thought there were negative signs. Scary how nerves can affect us when it comes to big decisions like marriage." *And babies.*

"I don't know why I'm letting everything get to me. That's not usually like me." Zoe wiped away a tear. "I love Sean, so why can't I plan my own wedding?"

"It's because it's *your* wedding, which makes it that much bigger of a deal." Jo gave her a quick hug. "Let's take your mind off your worries and go have some fun."

"Okay, and thank you both. Fun is exactly what I

need." Zoe shook out her hands. "I can't take anything else going wrong."

We snagged our men and walked around for an hour, sampling food and drinks and meeting all the psychics. It felt good not to have to work, but I was very interested in joining this organization. Everyone in town who was interested in getting a reading from me had already been to my sanctuary. I was just happy to meet like-minded people I could talk shop with, those who truly understood me. There were definitely a few fakes present, but overall, the rest of the psychics were the real deal.

I looked up ahead and saw a familiar looking man arguing with a woman. I nudged Jo. "Hey, isn't that Rich?" I pointed.

Jo shaded her eyes with her hand and squinted. "Yeah, that sure looks like him, but what is he doing with her?" She studied him closer.

"Oh, blimey. This is not what I need right now," Sean muttered under his breath, but I heard.

"What's wrong?" I asked.

"His ex is here, that's what's wrong," Mitch chimed in as he walked beside us, still holding Jeremiah who was also now sleeping in his obviously-more-capable-than-mine big, strong arms.

"What ex?" Zoe's forehead puckered with worry lines as she searched the crowd of people.

"You can't expect to be in Divinity and not run into one of Sean's exes." Cole leaned in from behind us.

"Yeah, but she's not just any ex." Jo sounded grim.

"What does that mean?" Zoe's worry frown turned into a scowl.

Biff, Cole's huge Great Dane, even let out a loud whoof.

"Looks like we're about to find out," I said, a

feeling of doom settling over me like a dark cloud of negative energy, crackling across the back of my neck.

Rich had stormed off before Jo could talk to him, and the blond goddess he'd been arguing with walked in our direction, her pale green eyes trained on Sean. She was probably the most beautiful woman I'd ever seen. Zoe let out a little gasp, and Sean took her hand in his.

"Well, if it isn't Sean O'Malley." Her gaze traveled the length of him as she tucked a strand of her thick long hair behind her ear. "I was wondering when I would run into you. It's been far too long since we've seen each other, darling. How've you been?"

"Engaged." Sean lifted Zoe's hand so her impressive engagement ring was clearly visible. "You?"

The goddess blinked, her lips parting momentarily until she regained her wits. She settled her gaze on Zoe, her eyelids closing a fraction as she looked her over. Zoe straightened her spine and stood there stiffly.

The woman held out her hand. "I'm Audra Grimshaw. I'm one of the psychics here." Her eyes were filled with devilish delight as she added, "I'm also Sean's *ex*-fiancé. I can only hope your engagement lasts longer than mine did."

Zoe's gaze cut to Sean's, and he closed his eyes briefly before glaring at Audra. It was clear he hadn't told his current fiancé he'd been engaged before. Not very smart. Sean was one of my best friends, and he hadn't told me either. He also hadn't told me he'd dated a woman who was psychic. I'd thought I was the first psychic in Divinity. I looked at Jo with raised eyebrows. She gave me a look that said I'll fill you in later.

"Zoe Burnham." Zoe ignored Audra's hand. "Your engagement didn't last because clearly you weren't the right woman for Sean." Zoe looked as if she'd grown a few inches as she added, "Make no mistake. I am." She might be a little softer than her cousin Jo, but that didn't mean she wasn't just as fierce when she needed to be.

Audra's face hardened a little as she dropped her outstretched empty palm. She inhaled a breath and opened her mouth as if she were about to say something more.

Sean put his arm around Zoe. "Can't say it was good seeing you, Audra. We're done here."

"On the contrary, my darling, we've only just begun." She turned around and walked away, hips swaying seductively with every step she took.

Zoe stepped out from under Sean's arm and away from him, crossing her arms over her chest. "Why didn't you tell me you were engaged before? And to a psychic? That was so embarrassing. I feel like a fool."

"It was a long time ago. She wasn't even a practicing psychic back then." His gaze cut to mine apologetically before sweeping back to Zoe's pleadingly. "We were young and stupid. She cheated on me, so I broke things off and vowed never to be vulnerable again. She moved away, and I was fine for years until you came along." He reached for her, but she stepped back again. "Don't you see how much more my proposal to you means because of that? I never planned to get engaged again, but you're everything to me, love."

"You still should have told me." Zoe walked away, and Sean started to follow. She whipped her head over her shoulder. "Don't. I need some time alone."

Sean heaved a heavy sigh as he watched her turn around and leave without once looking back.

"She's right. You should have told her." Jo patted

his back. "Don't worry. I'll talk to her." Jo hurried after Zoe.

I gave Sean a sympathetic look, glanced at Mitch apologetically, and then tried to catch up to Jo. I wasn't about to miss out on what was happening, and of course, be there to help Zoe.

For once the drama involved someone other than me.

WHAT SEEMED LIKE FOREVER LATER OF SEARCHING FOR Zoe and Jo, I gave up. They must have turned down another row, and I had ended up in the back of the fair near the woods. A feeling of being watched made goosebumps pop up on my arms, and my scalp prickle like needles in a pin cushion. A crow squawked, and I jumped. Scolding myself, I turned around and decided to make my way back to safer territory with people I knew and trusted.

"Congratulations."

I jerked to a stop, startled out of my thoughts. A little old woman with long gray hair in a bun and a scarf wrapped around her head smiled at me from beneath her tent. Blowing out a relieved beath, I took a few steps toward her, wondering how she knew I was a newlywed. Then I chuckled. Duh, this was a Psychic Fair, after all.

"Thank you," I replied. I had thought I'd met all the psychics, but I'd somehow missed her tent. It was on the edge of the park near the woods. "I'm Sunshine Stone, but you can call me Sunny."

"I know who you are, dearie." She took my hand in both of hers, and a warm, comfortable feeling swept through my veins like a familiar elixir. Her knowing gaze met mine, and she studied me closer. "Your ability is strong, but you haven't quite figured out how to read your visions, have you?"

"I'm getting there, but you're right. My visions always come true, but it sometimes takes me a bit to figure out what the visions are trying to tell me."

"Reading your visions is a skill that takes time." She looked me in the eye, her lavender gaze all-knowing and intense. "Talk to your grandmother. She'll help you."

My eyebrows drew together. "Granny Gert? But how...?"

"She too has the gift."

I sucked in a sharp breath. "Wait." My mouth fell open, and my eyes sprang wide. "My Grandmother Gertrude is psychic?" That would certainly explain a lot over the years, but why wouldn't she tell me? She knew how hard it had been with my parents being disappointed in me and getting others to believe in my gift. I was a little hurt and confused as to why she wouldn't want to help me.

"She's not a practicing psychic, but yes, she was born with the gift," the woman named Helga—according to her sign Helga's Hideaway—said. "I'm sure she might be a bit rusty because people our age didn't tell others back then. I refused to let that stop me." She rubbed her hand over mine and closed her eyes momentarily, then opened them with a smile. "You will pass the gift onto your child."

"Oh, boy." My heart flipped. "My husband won't want to hear that."

"He'll come around in time." She patted my hand with her wrinkled arthritic one. "You'll see."

"Well, it was great meeting you, but I should really get back to my party. I don't want them to worry about me." I let go of her hand, a little freaked out over our conversation. "And thank you for the congrats on my wedding." I started to leave.

"I didn't say congratulations because of your wedding."

My feet stopped moving, and I scratched my head as I looked back at her. "Then why the congrats?"

"For the baby you're carrying."

Crazy Lady say what? I thought as my hands dropped to my flat stomach which had turned over as if in protest. "But I'm not...."

"Yes, my dear, you are."

"But how?"

She arched a gray eyebrow high.

"I mean, I know how. I am married, after all, but *just* married. It's only been two months."

"Exactly."

"A honeymoon baby?" No, I couldn't be pregnant, could I?

I thought about the symptoms I'd been having. I was so tired and sick but only in the morning, then starving the rest of the day. I hadn't gone to see Doc Wilcox yet like I'd promised Mitch I would because I'd been too busy.

"Stranger things have happened." The woman cackled.

"A baby." I swallowed hard. "And it's psychic?"

"I didn't say this child."

I gaped. "You mean I'm having more than one child?"

"Time will tell, my dear. I've said enough." She flipped over an hour glass and disappeared behind the curtain in her tent, leaving me reeling from the impact of her words.

3

"What did Doc Wilcox say?" Mitch asked as he sat in the chair across from me at Smokey Jo's Tavern the next day. I didn't say anything last night because I'd wanted to be sure. When I woke up sick again this morning, Mitch insisted I cancel my readings and go see the doctor.

For once, I agreed.

"Well, I don't have the summer flu," I replied vaguely, still unsure how to tell him since I hadn't even wrapped my head around the idea yet. I'd asked him to meet me for lunch since he was working, and the police department was nearby.

His face paled, and he took my hands in his own. "Whatever it is, we'll get through it together."

"I certainly hope so." I laughed, strumming my fingers on his hand. Seventies folk music filtered through the sound system, and I tried to focus on that so I would stay centered and not have a panic attack.

"They've come a long way with modern medicine." He stilled my fingers, holding them gently in his big hands.

"Oh, trust me. I'm no martyr. I will be asking for all the drugs they'll give me." I willed the acid churning in my stomach to go away, taking deep breaths like I did when I meditated. "The thought of being in pain terrifies me," I admitted, wishing I could leave and go meditate now.

"Sunny, you're scaring me." A muscle in his jaw bulged as he paused a beat before asking, "Do you have a tumor growing inside you?"

I barked out a laugh, earning a few curious looks from the restaurant's patrons. "Oh, what's growing inside me is much bigger than a tumor." I shivered, hysteria bubbling just beneath the surface.

"Just tell me." He squeezed my hands. "I can take it."

"I don't have a tumor inside me." My gaze met his and locked. "I have a baby inside me. A baby that's probably going to be almost the size of the Sasquatch cubs."

His eyes widened and lips parted. "Y-You're pregnant?"

Hearing the word spoken out loud had my heart pumping as fast as Jackhammer Jeremiah's tiny feet. "Yes, and It's going to be huge, and what if it's two, and what if it's grumpy, and what if it's psychic and can hear my thoughts and knows I'll be terrible at this, and, and, and...it's all your fault!" I burst into tears.

The clanging of silverware and dishes and conversation ceased. All eyes turned toward our table with knowing looks of pity, which made me cry harder.

"The honeymoon is *not* over," I blubbered at them all, wiping my running nose and shooing them back to their own business.

"Sunny, I...I don't know what to say." He held up his hands, his head shaking and face a shade paler than normal.

Wrong answer. "Well, that's a fine how do you do." I glared at him. "Isn't that just dandy?"

"No, no, don't get me wrong. *I'm* happy, I am. I'm just confused because clearly, *you're* not. Frankly, I don't know what to do about that." He dropped his hands to the table, staring at his fork then finally meeting my gaze. "I thought this was what you wanted?"

"It is. I mean it was. That was before I realized bear cubs don't like me." I started bawling again. "What if they roar or one can read my mind? They'll hate me. Granny Gert probably knew all along but didn't tell me like the gray lady said."

"I honestly don't have a clue what you're talking about." He rubbed his whiskered jaw, his eyes darting all over the place as if searching for something.

My eyes hardened. "Why'd you have to be so big? Mitchell Michael Stone, what were you thinking?" I wailed harder.

"I'm thinking I don't speak pregnant. Does Rosetta Stone have a version for that language, cuz I'm lost, babe?"

"Don't you babe me." I thrust my finger in his direction, pointing at him and then wagging it. "You know what you did."

Jo marched over to our table with hands on her hips, looking like the fierce Amazon queen that she was. Her eyelids reduced to slits as she stared at my husband in true best friend fashion. "Start talking, Mitch. What did you do?"

He held up his hands. "I know my rights. I plead the fifth." He pushed his chair back, surged up and headed straight for the rich mahogany bar.

"And where do you think you're going, buddy?"

Zoe asked as she passed by him with an accusatory expression.

"I'm no rookie." He stared at all of us with a crazed look in his eye. "I'm calling for backup."

"Wise choice, Detective," Jo growled like a true mama bear defending her cub. "You're gonna need it."

I watched Mitch make a beeline for the stools at the end, as far away from us as he could get. Cole and Sean joined him and all three bent their heads in deep conversation, looking up every now and then as if they were staring at a group of aliens.

"All right, people, nothing more to see here." Jo waved her hands until everyone returned to their conversations, finishing their lunches.

"Are you okay?" Zoe asked, taking a seat at the table.

"No, yes...I don't know." I blew my nose.

Jo rubbed my back. "You can tell us anything, you know."

"I'm pregnant." My eyes filled with more tears I obviously had zero control over. "And I'm afraid I'm going to be a horrible mother."

Surprise then knowing looks passed between my besties, followed quickly by hugs and squeals of joy.

"You are going to be an amazing mother, Sunny." Jo clapped her hands. "I'm so happy for you and Mitch."

"What was I thinking?" I said, blowing into a hankie. "I'm a horrible godmother. How am I supposed to know what to do as a mom? Meanwhile, Grumpy Pants didn't even want kids, yet he's Super Godfather to your twins already. How is that possible?"

"You will know what to do when the time comes," Zoe chimed in. "Remember, Jo was worried she would be a bad mother because she wasn't very good with

Biff, yet look at her now. She's an amazing fur mommy and a pro with the twins. I think every woman feels like that at first. I know I sure wouldn't be ready right now."

"Trust me, I'm not." I obviously wasn't a good fur mommy to Morty, either, with the way he'd been acting lately. I dropped my head to my hands, took a deep breath, and tried to recenter and ground myself. I had to pull myself together.

"But you *will* be ready. You're just getting used to the idea because you got pregnant so quickly. I know about surprised pregnancies, believe me." Jo took my hand. "This is a good thing, Sunny."

"You're right." A calm settled over me when I really thought about having a baby. For the first time, a seed of excitement sprouted in my gut. "I'm going to be a mom," I half whispered in awe, amazed at the turn of my emotions.

At least crime in Divinity was pretty slow right now, so the police department didn't need my help, and my husband could relax. It was a good time to be pregnant, I supposed, finally wrapping my head around the idea.

"Wow, pregnancy hormones are no joke." Zoe looked at me, her gaze a little freaked out, but she couldn't stop eyeing me in fascination.

"No kidding," I agreed, then my eyes met Jo's mischievous gaze. "Is it like this for all nine months?"

Jo laughed. "Oh, ladies, you have no idea."

IT WAS SUNDAY NIGHT, THE LAST NIGHT OF THE PHYSIC Fair. The evening was a warm one, the stars hidden beneath the overcast sky, but pretty much everyone in town was here. My family was thrilled over the idea of a baby, giving loads of unsolicited advice while arguing over whose advice was better. They were babysitting the twins to give us all a much-needed night out without babies or any talk of them.

Meanwhile, Mitch was an over protective mess half the time, fussing over me nonstop, not letting me lift a finger and trying to make me eat twenty-four-seven. The other half of the time, he eyed me warily, afraid of what personality might emerge next. I seriously needed a distraction before they all drove me crazy for real. My hormones had already done a decent job of doing just that, but my family was on the verge of pushing me over the edge.

"There they are." I headed in the direction of Jo, Cole, Sean and Zoe. They stood by the food and beverage tent. Jo and Cole were arm-in-arm while Zoe and Sean were an arm's length apart. At least they were there together, so that was a step in the right direction.

I just hoped the drama was done.

Mitch grabbed my hand. "Slow down, you might trip."

I held my breath and counted to ten as I lectured myself not to go sybil on him. "I have sneakers on, *honey*, and the ground is level here," I said carefully. "I'm fine."

"I'm not taking any chances, babe." He gripped my hand more firmly as if I were a child about to bolt, or throw a temper tantrum. I had to admit both were a distinct possibility if he didn't knock it off.

"I'm sorry, Rich," Jo said to the man who had joined their group. "I have a business to run, and Sean caught you making too many mistakes."

"Come on, Mrs. West," he pleaded, running a hand

over his bald head, then down over his jet-black goatee. "Give me another chance, and I won't let you down. I need this. Word of mouth is everything, and your business can put my winery on the map. If you fire me as a distributor and word gets out, you'll ruin me."

"You heard her, Hastings. The answer is no." Sean took a step toward Jo. "You've gotta get your act together, lad. That's no way to run a business."

"This is all your fault." Rich walked past Sean and clenched his fists, his boots kicking up dust. "You're gonna regret this. I'm going to see to it myself." The wind picked up, swirling the dirt around.

"You do that," Sean hollered after him, throwing his hands up in the air. "I'm just doing my job. How is that my fault?" He looked at Zoe.

"Honey, I didn't say that it was." She glanced at Jo and me, then shrugged, looking a little helpless.

"I'm getting a drink. Anyone want anything?" Sean looked around at all of us, stress deepening the crow's feet at the corners of his baby blues.

I would have to meditate with him soon.

Mitch and Cole glanced at Jo and me, then each other. No words were necessary. They followed Sean to the beverage tent in true three-musketeers fashion.

"I thought you two were better?" Jo asked Zoe.

"So did I, but as soon as we got here, we saw Audra again. A tension settled between us we haven't been able to shake." Her face fell. "This doesn't look good."

Just then, Mark rounded the corner. Mark and Rich were both in their thirties and had met at the horse races in Saratoga. Mark came to a stop by Jo. "Hey, Jo, did Rich talk to you yet? He's worried about messing up."

"Yes, but unfortunately, I had to let him go."

Mark's face fell. "Are you sure I can't change your mind? The guy really could use a break. He's been down on his luck lately."

"I gave him a break, Mark." Jo winced. "I'm sorry, but I can't afford to change my mind."

"Understood." Mark nodded, letting out a deep sigh. "Thanks for giving him a shot in the first place."

"You're welcome. I really do wish him the best."

Mark's gaze cut to Zoe's. He had dark blonde Ken Doll hair, perfectly styled and slicked back in place. His face was clean-shaven and jawline chiseled. He was a handsome man, but as different from Sean as he could be.

"It's great to see you, Zoe," Mark's voice dipped warmly and his gaze softened. "You look beautiful as always."

Zoe's face flushed pink, and she fidgeted, shifting her stance as if uncomfortable. "Thank you, Mark. I hope you've been well."

His gaze stayed glued to her face, but his honey tone hardened slightly and body stiffened a little. "I've been better."

Sean and the guys returned from the tent, with Sean making a beeline straight for Zoe and wrapping his arm around her. "Silverman."

"O'Malley." Mark nodded his head once, then glanced at his watch, back to business mode. "Catch you guys later. I have to see a man about a horse, literally. Antonio Ventura's horse is lame, and with the upcoming race in Saratoga, time is of the essence." He headed over to a short, stocky, salt and pepper haired man in jeans and a western shirt, who looked to be in his fifties.

"Antonio Ventura?" I asked, not having seen him before.

"His family owns Dolce Vita Stables," Mitch responded. "Silverman is their vet. Nice family. He doesn't come into town that often except for things like the festivals, but you've probably seen his wife, Olivia. She loves Divinity and frequents it often."

Recognition dawned. They were somewhat celebrities around Divinity. "I've heard of them. Don't their horses win a lot?"

"They sure do." Admiration laced Zoe's voice. "A horse coming up lame is a serious thing. I'm sure Mark can help him. He's an amazing vet."

"Hmmm," was all Sean said.

"He *is* an amazing vet," Zoe responded.

"That you use to date," Sean added.

Zoe crossed her arms. "At least I wasn't engaged to him."

"There's nothing going on between us. I promise you." Sean took her hands in his own, looking frustrated and worried. "You believe me, don't you?"

"I—"

"You scumbag. How dare you." A man charged forward toward Sean, anger rolling off him in a wave the size of a tsunami. He was tall and built, nearly as big as Sasquatch, with curly fawn-brown hair.

Cole took a step forward with balled fists, but Mitch stopped him. Thunder rolled and lightning cracked in the distance. The fireworks were bound to be cancelled with the storm moving in early, and the storm standing before Sean screamed clear and present danger.

Sean held his hands up. "Easy, lad, I have no idea who you are?"

"The name's Greg Gates."

"Sorry, pal, it's not ringing a bell. I'm Sean O'Malley."

"I know who you are." The man ground his teeth.

"I'm sorry, but I *don't* know you."

"I'm the man whose girlfriend you slept with."

All heck broke loose at once....

Audra appeared from out of nowhere.

Greg took a swing at Sean.

Sean threatened Audra.

Zoe stormed off.

Rain came down in droves.

Everyone dashed for their cars.

The night couldn't possibly get any worse....

4

"Have you heard the news?" Lulubelle—our town's resident gossip, head of the Bunco Babes, and wife to Big Don of Big Don's Auto—blurted as she burst through the door of Pump Up the Volume hair salon and spa. Her teased blond hair was glued in place.

Jo and I had taken Zoe to the salon this morning for a girl's day to get our hair and nails done. The room oozed comfort and class. Overstuffed chairs to sit on, cucumber or lemon water to sip, the latest magazines to read, soothing sounds of nature to relax to, and therapeutic smells to boggle the senses.

After last night, she needed the distraction to take her mind off her fight with Sean. Then we were supposed to have lunch at the inn with my mother, Granny Gert, Fiona and Great-Grandma Tootsie. They'd kept the twins overnight, and we were picking them up at noon. It was amazing what a difference twenty-four hours could make. Jo looked rested and refreshed.

Zoe, on the other hand, looked to be a stressed-out mess.

"What on earth is wrong with you, woman?"

Raoulle the stylist snapped. "You can't come in here shrieking like that. My Lord, you just took ten years off my life and nearly twice as many hairs off my poor client's head."

I could attest to that. Raoulle used to be the shampoo guy but had been promoted to stylist. The man was dangerous with a pair of scissors when he got worked up. Last time he'd cut my hair, I was left with bald patches and in need of a wig. I shuddered from the memory.

"Well, out with it, now that you've got us all worked up." He waved his scissors about, and his client ducked.

Smart woman.

Belle took a moment to catch her breath, her cherubic cheeks and triple chins jiggling. "Audra Grimshaw is dead," she finally got out between breaths.

Raoulle let out a shriek that sent a flock of birds outside the window squawking high in the cloudy sky, and a chunk of his client's hair falling to the floor.

The room gasped.

Zoe covered her gaping mouth, unable to speak.

Jo wrapped her arms around her, at a loss for words as well.

"What happened?" I asked, because clearly everyone else had lost their minds.

"No one knows for sure." Belle shook her hair-spray-frozen head of hair. "She was found late last night by Detective Fuller when he was making his rounds after the storm. He found her in the parking lot of Mini Central Park in a puddle of water by her car. The storm had knocked down a power line, and she was electrocuted." Belle placed her hand over her heart. "Isn't that just awful? Bless her heart."

"So, it was an accident, then, right?" Zoe asked.

"Not according to Coroner Kip Johnson. The results of the autopsy aren't in yet, but word is, she showed signs of a struggle before dying of electrocution." If anyone knew any inside scoop, it was Belle. She locked eyes with Zoe. "They're not ruling out murder."

"Oh, no, not again." Jo looked at me with dread filling her eyes.

I needed to speak with Mitch asap. No words were necessary for us all to know Sean threatened Audra in front of the whole town, then the storm hit and everyone left. Zoe had told us Sean didn't come home last night. The unspoken question was where did he go and does he have an alibi.

Because it was beginning to look like he needed one.

———

THE DIVINITY POLICE PRECINCT WAS BUZZING WITH activity. The psychics, venders and patrons were all ordered not to leave town until they had been cleared by the police. The police were in the process of questioning everyone and taking statements when I arrived. Zoe and Jo had gone on to the inn while I headed straight to my detective husband.

"Oh, no you don't," Mitch said when I walked into the meeting room. "Turn right around and go see your parents like you had planned, Tink. We've got things covered here."

"That's right, Detective," Chief Spencer chimed in. He was an older clone of Mitch and treated him like a son. He didn't believe in my abilities either. "We don't need any consulting on this case."

"Now, hold on," Mayor Cromwell added his two cents. "Ms. Meadows has proven to be a valuable asset in the past."

"*Mrs. Stone*," Mitch responded, "is too close to this case since Sean O'Malley is one of her best friends."

Mayor Cromwell, who had never been a fan of my husband but adored me, pointed his stubby finger in Mitch's face. "Look here, Stone. We have a town full of people and a dead body. We need all the help we can get."

Captain Grady Walker held up his hands, looking more authoritative than ever. "Calm down, gentlemen. Given that Sunny is a psychic and this is a Psychic Fair, we could use her help more than ever in getting the other psychics to open up."

He was a distinguished gentleman in his seventies, still impressive with his tall height, bald head and silver goatee. I could see why Granny Gert swooned every time he was in her presence. He'd turned down promotions in the past because he preferred to be in on the action, but even he had mentioned this might be his last year on the force. He'd earned his retirement years ago but never had a reason to retire.

That was before Granny Gert moved to Divinity.

"Now, wait just a minute, Captain." Mitch stood. "Sunny can't possibly work in her condition."

I let out an exasperated *ugh* and plopped my hands on my hips. "I'm pregnant, not incapacitated. There's no reason I can't be a consultant if it will help clear Sean's name. And by the way, he's one of your best friend's too, yet you're still on the case."

"It's my job."

I straightened my shoulders, trying to stand as tall as I could. "And *my* job is to see who's telling the truth, and who might be hiding something."

The room grew quiet for several moments.

"Sorry, Detective," Captain Walker finally said. "Sunny stays."

"Okay, Captain, bring us up to speed on where we're at?" Chief Spencer crossed his arms, all business and clearly over the Sunny and Mitch show.

For once, we were on the same page.

I pulled my handy dandy notebook out of my fringed satchel and ignored the eye roll of a certain detective as he reached into his sport coat and pulled out his own notebook. We all sat around the table in the center of the room and waited as Captain Walker looked through his notes.

"Sean O'Malley is our main suspect. He was once engaged to Audra Grimshaw, and everyone in town saw him get into a fight with her current boyfriend, Greg Gates. Audra tried to break it up, and Sean threatened her. He said, and I quote, 'Stay away from me and my fiancé, or you'll be sorry.'" The captain's eyes locked with mine.

I looked at Mitch, but neither one of us had anything to add.

"Unfortunately, Sean doesn't have an alibi," the captain continued. "He was seen at Gretta's Grocery buying a case of beer late last night. Then he took off and no one saw him until today. He says he parked on a back road where he got drunk and passed out until morning and then came back to the shocking news. The question is, did he return to the park and confront Audra before she left and then head to the back road to get drunk after realizing what he'd done? The coroner saw signs of a struggle, but the cause of death was electrocution."

"Sean O'Malley isn't capable of murder. He's a

lover not a fighter. You all know that," I pleaded with them, but even I knew things didn't look good for him.

"That's your opinion," Mitch said, tapping his pen on the meeting table. "While I happen to agree with it, this just shows you're not looking at the facts and remaining objective."

Mayor Cromwell shot Mitch a warning look.

Mitch shrugged but didn't say anything more. Smart husband, I thought, if he wanted the honeymoon to last. But I couldn't deny he was right. I had to stay focused and remain objective. The truth always came out eventually. In the meantime, I planned to follow the evidence to the real killer.

"What about Rich Hastings?" I asked, steering the conversation back on the case and off of me. "We saw him arguing with Audra the first night we were here. Maybe someone should see what that was about."

"That's true," Mitch admitted. "We did see that."

"Good, add that to your list," Captain walker responded.

"What else you got, Captain?" Chief Spencer asked.

"Well, then there's the deceased's boyfriend. Greg Gates suspected Audra of cheating on him. Since she had a past with Sean, he accused her of cheating on him with Sean. After the storm hit and everyone left, he could have gone back to confront Audra. No one has found him to question him yet."

"I'm on it, Sir." Mitch wrote in his notebook.

"Good. And while you're doing that, I would like Sunny to talk to the psychics." Mitch's head snapped up, but the captain's gaze never left mine as he continued. "Willow Goodbody has been a rival psychic to Audra for years, always in competition to outdo her.

She's a person of interest. I'd really like to hear what she has to say about Audra's death."

"You got it, Sir." I wrote in my own notebook, ignoring the grunt from Detective Grumpy Pants beside me.

"I would also like someone to do some digging into Audra's whereabouts and phone messages. If she was having an affair, and it wasn't with Sean, then let's see if we can find out who it was with. Maybe they had a reason for wanting the affair kept quiet."

"Done." Mitch added another note.

"Sunny, while you're talking to the psychics, see if you can find out the people who had a reading done by Audra." Captain Walker checked his notes again. "Maybe she had a disgruntled client who didn't like what they heard."

"Done," I mimicked, earning a frown from my husband.

"I think that's enough to get started, people." Chief Spencer stood. "Let me know if Detective Fuller finds out anything more from the people he's taking statements from. I'd like to wrap this murder up before the rest of the summer events. The last thing Divinity needs is another scandal."

"That's for sure." Mayor Cromwell shook his large head, his crazy red troll hair bouncing wildly. "Divinity can't afford any more ruined festivals. I have faith Ms...er, Sunny, will shed some light on the clues needed to solve this mystery."

"Thank you, Mayor. I'll do my best." I smiled.

"Excuse me while I take my *wife* for lunch." Mitch wrapped his hand around my arm and stood. "She is eating for two, you know."

"Maybe three," I muttered.

"What's that?" he asked as we walked out of the precinct.

"Look at that tree," I replied. "Isn't it pretty?"

He glanced at the basic Oak tree that hadn't changed a bit since he'd moved to Divinity, then back at me with an intense gaze. "Yeah, we need to get some food into you asap. You're delirious."

This time I rolled *my* eyes. "I'm not delirious, but I am hungry. I know a place that's divine."

"Yeah, where?"

"The inn."

He stopped walking and stared at me. "Since when do you want to go to your parents' place?"

"Since Great-Grandma Tootsie makes the best Reuben sandwiches. Blame it on pregnancy cravings." I smiled innocently.

He waited a beat, but let the matter go.

My husband knew me so well. He knew I was up to something. He just didn't know what. I really did have a craving. A craving for a conversation with a certain psychic named Willow Goodbody. Jo and Zoe had texted me that she'd checked into the inn while they were there for lunch, but a certain detective didn't need to know that.

We got in the car, and he started the engine. Before we left the parking lot, he reached over and tugged on my seatbelt. Twice. I looked out the window and groaned.

It was going to be a long nine months.

AFTER LUNCH MITCH HAD LEFT TO TRACK DOWN GREG Gates while I claimed I was tired and going to take a nap at the inn. Really, I just needed him gone so I could question Willow without him hovering over me. To my disappointment, Willow had stepped out. I wasn't up for a nap, but I could always use a good meditation session.

First, I needed to set the proper mood. I chose the back patio. It was a gorgeous day with the sun shining off the lake and the breeze rustling the leaves on the trees. Birds chirped and grasshoppers hummed. Nature's meditation music. No one was in the backyard, so it was the perfect time to enjoy peace and quiet and block out any stimuli.

Meditation was the perfect tool when I needed a break from a stressful day—in my case several stressful days—to gather my bearings and ground myself back in the present. In my Sanctuary, I carved out time each day so my brain and body became accustomed to clearing my mind and relaxing, but in a pinch, I could make do with my surroundings.

There was no one way to correctly meditate, but using certain tools like Mala prayer beads could help. It didn't matter what religion a person was, the beads simply helped them to focus on their meditation and keep track of their repetitions as they moved from one bead to the next. Since I didn't have my beads with me, I would rely on Mudras.

It had been a while since I'd used hand gestures to channel energy. Different combinations of movement impacted the body in different ways. I wiggled my fingers, much like a pianist before a concerto, focusing on what each digit represented. The thumb was fire, the index finger air, the middle finger space, the ring finger earth and the little finger water. All elements must be in equilibrium in order to enjoy a balanced life.

This was the perfect meditation for me today because I was anything but balanced.

My anxiety over becoming a mother made me feel weak. I needed to be strong if I was going to help Sean clear his name. I sat down on the center of the patio in a full lotus position, crossing my legs pretzel style with my feet on top of my knees. I chose the Prithvi mudra to increase my strength. By joining my thumb and ring finger, I activated fire and earth, channeling fire energy with the rigidity and grounding earth force. This combination would help me to harness the power of fire in a structured way so that it could help me grow and become strong rather than let my anxiety overwhelm me.

I kept my other fingers straight to provide a clear message to the universe about which elements to activate. I sat with my head, neck, and spine in proper alignment. Releasing the tension, I relaxed my muscles, closed my eyes, and breathed slowly in and out through my nostrils. Clearing my mind, I felt the energy vibrate through my body.

Suddenly, my mind's eye narrowed into tunnel vision just like it always did whenever I had a vision. I felt the pain of labor. I smelled the antiseptic of a hospital room. I heard a heartbeat. Relief washed over me when the pain left. I heard the crying of babies. I felt joy, then surprise, then confusion. Babies? There were two babies. Twins? Maybe. Maybe not. My heart started pounding, and my breathing grew choppy. One thing was certain....

Something was wrong.

"There you are," Granny Gert's voice snapped me out of my vision. "We've been looking everywhere for you."

"Here I am." I opened my eyes, more confused than ever.

"Are you okay, dear? You look vexed."

"I'm fine." I tried to regulate my breathing and heartbeat back to normal.

"Let me help you up, dear." She held out a hand and helped me get to my feet. "We'd better get back to the dining room before your mother calls in the National Guard. I wouldn't put anything past her now that she has a grandbaby on the way."

Maybe grandbabies, I thought, but didn't say a word. I just followed her back to the dining room until we were seated, and she'd poured me some tea.

Some things were better left unsaid.

5

"Why didn't you tell me you're psychic?" I finally asked Granny Gert as we sat at the dining room table of the inn, sipping our tea. This much-needed conversation was long overdue, and I wanted to take my mind off more disturbing matters like two babies and my pet cat who didn't seem to want anything to do with me.

Granny Gert's snappy brown eyes filled with compassion and understanding. She patted her snow-white hair that she had Raoulle wash and set once a week down at the salon. It had turned pure white when she was sixteen, from Scarlet Fever, and she hadn't colored it since. People envied her hair, including Captain Walker. My grandmother was still a beautiful woman and just as sweet on the inside.

"I didn't say anything because I wasn't sure the things I saw were really visions, my dear. Back in the day, people would have strung me up for being a witch or locked me in a loony bin for talk like that. I guess I got used to keeping my mouth closed and never learned how to develop my skills." She reached out and took my hand into her brown spotted one and held on tight. "Your gift is special, Sunny. Don't ever let anyone tell you otherwise."

"I won't." I hugged her. "I'm glad we can talk about this. I mean, I always knew I could talk to you about anything. I just wasn't sure you could fully understand. Now, I know better. There's still time for you to develop your gift, too."

"Oh, go on with you now. You can't teach an old bird like me new tricks." The mischievous twinkle I so loved was back in her eye.

"You're not old." Great-Grandma Tootsie brought out a plate of baklava from the kitchen and set it on the table. "Why, you're a spring chicken compared to me."

"And you're a beautiful anomaly," I said, diving into the dessert.

Morty appeared from around the corner. I reached for him, but he backed away and jumped into Great-Grandma Tootsie's lap.

"Will you look at that?" Granny Gert said. "That little devil used to be my shadow. Looks like I've been replaced as well."

"Maybe he's jealous of you flirting with Captain Walker like he is of me with Mitch." I set down my fork, my appetite gone. "I don't know what's wrong with him. He's just not himself these days."

"I wouldn't worry so much. Morty's a gentleman," Great-Grandma Tootsie said. "He knows you two already have eyes for other fellas. I'm sure that's why he's giving me so much attention these days. He'll come around in no time. You'll see."

"I sure hope so." I sighed.

Fiona joined us at the table, fashionably dressed in a summer jumper and looking much younger than her eighty years. "What'd I miss."

"Nothing, Ms. Prima Donna." Granny Gert shook her head as Fiona preened, ignoring the insult.

"Just Morty's odd behavior, and my pregnancy fears, and then there's the murder investigation. I've been so stressed lately, Doc Wilcox suggested I meditate. The problem is, every time I meditate, I have a vision. I keep seeing two babies," I admitted. "Then Helga of Helga's Hideaway said something about a second child. We only heard one heartbeat at the doctor's office, and it's too soon to have a sonogram yet. The visions are very confusing, and I get the sense that something is wrong." I sipped my tea before asking, "Do you think I could be having twins?"

"Twins?" My mother came running into the living room, followed by my father and Harry. "Donald, did you hear that? There's two babies."

I set my cup down. "Mom, I didn't say that. I—"

"Where are the cigars, Harry," my father boomed. "We need to celebrate."

"Donald, don't you dare," My mother lectured.

"Wait, it's too soon to te—" I tried again, regretting my impulsive decision to tell them about my visions.

"Follow me, my friend." Harry led the way to the sidebar with gusto. "I make a mean Manhattan."

"Ohhh, I love a good martini." Fiona hustled after Harry, twittering, "It's happy hour somewhere."

"Where's the boy when we need him?" My father looked around.

"Still a newlywed," Harry chuckled.

"Boys oh day." Great-Grandma Tootsie headed for the kitchen while humming show tunes, Morty following her every step. "I'd better make some snacks."

Granny looked at me and jerked her head in the direction of the front door. "Hurry and make your escape while you still can. I have a feeling you're about to get the answers you seek. I'll cover for you."

Just then Willow Goodbody walked into the inn. I glanced back at my grandmother, but she had joined the others with her back to me. Hmmm, something told me she *saw* things just fine.

Too old my foot.

I HURRIED INTO THE LOBBY AND INTERCEPTED WILLOW. "Ms. Goodbody, it's lovely to see you again." I'd met her at the Psychic Fair on the first night. "I'm so glad you've chosen to stay at my parents' inn."

She was around the same age as Audra, but she was as dark as Audra was fair, and exotic looking, with rich chocolate curls, creamy cocoa eyes and the longest eyelashes I had ever seen. She stared at me for a long moment and then hoisted her chin a notch. "Mrs. Stone, I already talked to the police."

"I'm not the police, Willow. May I call you Willow?"

She nodded slowly, eying me with undeniable intelligence and something more.

"Please, call me Sunny," I continued. "I just wanted to talk to you. One psychic to another. I don't get to do that very often."

The tension left her shoulders, and she relaxed a little. "Sure."

"Great." I glanced back at the chaos still taking place in the living room. "Let's sit on the patio. It's such a beautiful day outside."

Once we were seated with a pitcher of lemonade, I smiled. "So, tell me, how did you like Divinity's first Psychic Fair?"

"It was eventful, to say the least."

"I know. Poor Audra. To die in such a horrible way is awful."

"I agree that the way she died is awful, but I can't say that I will miss her."

"I take it you're not a fan of hers." I took a sip of lemonade.

"No, I was not, as I'm sure you already know, Mrs. Stone." She set her glass down untouched. "I thought you wanted to talk. Not interrogate me."

"I'm sorry, you're right. I did know that, but I promise you, I do want to hear your side of the story." I pulled out my notebook. "From what I could see, Audra wasn't a very pleasant person."

"She was downright terrible." Willow shook her head. "We're all a part of the same psychic community, but Audra turned everything into a competition. Instead of working together to help people, she didn't care what she had to do to steal clients from others. She went as far as to say I was a fake." A look of hatred hardened Willow's face. "Audra Grimshaw crossed the line this time. I didn't kill her, but you can bet I had words with her."

"I imagine you were upset over losing clients to her." I looked up from my notebook.

"I was, but I met a man who made me feel better last night. He bought me a drink. Dawson Jones was his name. He's a handsome mechanic who liked the reading I gave for him. I predicted he would have a fantastic night if he played his cards right, and he did." A smile hovered over her sensual lips. "I'm sure he'll verify my story, since you're obviously fishing for an alibi. I'm hardly forgettable."

My cheeks flushed with heat. "I'll check on that and get back to you." I cleared my throat.

Dawson looked a lot like my husband and had a thing for me when he used to work for Big Don. He'd fixed my VW Bug many times. My radar for guys hitting on me was nonexistent. I'd had no idea he was flirting with me back then, and I'd accidentally shot him down. Then he was wrongly accused of tampering with my wedding.

Looked like he'd recovered just fine.

"I wasn't the only one upset about losing clients to her," Willow added, snapping me back to the case at hand. "A woman named Rita Haynes came storming into her tent on Sunday morning because some of her clients cancelled with her to see Audra instead."

"Ah, yes, I've heard of Rita." I searched my memory. "I believe she's a mental health therapist here in Divinity."

"Well, she was having a spell of her own. She made it clear she doesn't believe in psychic ability and accused Audra of preying on the mentally ill. I don't blame the woman for being mad. We're supposed to let people come to us, but Audra scours every town we're in to recruit people to come to her tent. It's just not right."

"No, I don't suppose it is."

"If we're finished here, I'd like to go to my room." Willow stood. "It's been an exhausting couple of days."

"Yes, it has," I agreed and stood as well. "Thank you for being honest with me. You've actually been a big help."

And now I had a new person of interest.

"THANK YOU FOR SEEING ME ON SUCH SHORT NOTICE," I said the next day as I sat on the couch in an office not that much different from my Sanctuary.

The room was painted a soft blue, with tranquil music playing, comfy furniture and serene paintings meant to put people at ease. Rita Haynes might not believe in psychics, but we weren't all that different in our desire to help others.

"No problem, Ms.," she checked her clipboard then looked up at me and smiled with kindness in her hazel eyes, "Meadows. How can I help you?"

I'd purposely used my maiden name because I didn't want to scare her off if she figured out I was married to Detective Stone. "Please, call me Sunny."

"Okay, Sunny." She tucked a strand of honey colored hair behind her ear and sat back in her chair. She looked to be in her fifties, with a nurturing vibe rolling off her in gentle waves. "Why don't you start by telling me what's troubling you."

"Well, I'm pregnant." That was the truth. I had really come to question her about Audra's murder, but now that I was actually here, I was kind of glad. It was nice to talk to someone who was impartial about my fears. It wasn't the first time I had ever talked to a therapist. I believed most people could benefit from therapy. But I hadn't talked to one since moving to Divinity. That was really surprising, now that I thought about it, given all I had been through in the last year and a half.

"I see, and being pregnant bothers you?"

"No, I mean it did at first, but not now." That was also true. "It didn't really *bother* me. It's more like it scared me."

"Does this have anything to do with your own mother?"

I blinked. Where had that come from?

"I don't think so," I answered. I thought about my ongoing strained relationship with my mother and started to look at things differently. "Actually, maybe this does have to do with my mother. I know my mother loves me, but she hasn't always been the best at showing me." My truest statement yet.

"And now you're afraid you won't be a good mother because you didn't have a good role model yourself."

"Possibly. I mean, my mother was an esteemed, tough lawyer, and my father was a world-renowned cardiologist. They had me later in life. I'm an only child. They didn't exactly have a lot of time to parent, but my grandmother was the best. Still is."

"Hmmm, and how does your mother feel about that?"

I barked out a laugh. "Let's just say it doesn't exactly give her the warm fuzzies."

"Does the baby's father have parents?"

"Not living."

"So maybe you're worried you will only have your grandmother to help you know what to do with your own baby, and she's getting older."

"Exactly. She's no spring chicken. If anything happens to her, I'm in big trouble. That and then there's the fact that my husband is a large man. I'm terrified I won't be able to carry his baby."

"You would be surprised what the human body is capable of." She patted my hand and made me feel so reassured. For a moment, I forgot why I was really in her office. "The mind and body are very connected. Most people don't realize how much so. If you start believing in yourself, your body will follow suit."

"I keep seeing two babies, so what if I'm having twins? I doubt my body will be up for that."

A palpable tension suddenly filled the room.

"What do you mean you keep seeing?" Her smile evaporated; her lips forming a thin, flat line.

Whoops.

"I mean, like in my dreams."

"What did you say your husband's name was?"

"I didn't." I gnawed at the inside of my cheek.

"I heard the detective was married to a psychic, but I didn't think he would stoop so low as to invade my place of business to try and get information out of me."

"Oh, trust me, he wouldn't. I would. I mean I wouldn't say I'm invading your business just to get information out of you. Everything I've told you is true. I've tried mediation, but that's what keeps triggering the visions."

"I don't believe in visions, *Mrs. Stone*, and I don't believe you." She clipped her pen back to her clipboard, the comforting therapist all but vanished, replaced by a vengeful woman. "You're sneaky, just like *her*."

"You mean Audra Grimshaw? I heard she stole your clients. I would never do something like that."

"No, you just stole my time. Time I could have spent helping people who actually need it." She stood.

"Believe me, I need all the help I can get." I grabbed my fringed cross-shoulder bag and stood as well. "I'm just trying to find out the truth."

"You want the truth? The truth is you people don't care about helping people. You only want their money. It's disgraceful to prey on vulnerable people by telling them what you think they want to hear, only to have them end up making the worst decisions of their lives.

Poor Ginger and Honey Lowenthal are perfect examples of that."

"Who are they?"

"My former clients, same as you." She walked over and opened her office door. "You can leave now, Mrs. Stone. And don't bother coming back."

"Do you have an alibi for Sunday night?" I said as I hurried out her office door before she could shove me out.

"You can ask my lawyer. I'm done talking."

"For someone who didn't do anything wrong, you seem a bit too angry and in need of therapy yourself."

She just glared at me silently, then proceeded to slam the door in my face.

The visit wasn't a total waste. She had helped me even if she didn't know it. She'd made me realize I needed to finally make peace with my mother, and maybe I wasn't having two babies. Maybe my visions were trying to tell me something else. Like the names of my newest suspects, Ginger and Honey.

The Lowenthal twins.

6

"Hi, Natalie. I'll have my usual." I took a seat at the bar in Warm Beginnings & Cozy Endings Café. I was starving after I left Rita Haynes office, so I'd headed straight to the café. Natalie's cooking was a close second to Great-Grandma Tootsie's.

The smells of cappuccinos and cocoas and teas mixed with sandwiches and burgers and desserts had my stomach growling so loud a few heads turned in my direction. I felt my cheeks flush and was sure my face must be as pink as the cupcake I was eyeing. Forcing my gaze away from the dessert case, I glanced around the café. All the buildings in Divinity were decorated with a theme. This café had a coffee theme, with a cream-swirled floor, making the atmosphere warm and cozy, hence the name. Today, it was busier than usual, with so many people having to stay in town until their names were cleared.

"Hi, Sunny, it's great to see you." Natalie Kirsch, the owner, smiled warmly.

She was about my age, with russet brown wavy hair and eyes. For a while, when my mother had favored her over me, like she did with pretty much everyone, I had unfairly disliked Natalie. Once I got to know her, we had become good friends.

"I'll be right back with your order and a little surprise," she added before disappearing into the kitchen.

Natalie was Sam the baker's daughter, but she'd wanted to make it on her own by opening her own café instead of working for him in the family bakery. Frankly, I was thrilled. Her Turkey Club sandwiches were to die for. She reappeared with one hand behind her back and set that very sandwich before me, which had my mouth watering something fierce. Poor Mitch was still the cook in our family, so eating out was a regular occurrence for us. Now that I was pregnant, I needed to learn how to cook. Maybe Natalie would give me some pointers.

"I heard congratulations are in order." She set the pink cupcake on a celebration plate before me, wiped her hands on a dishrag and then slung it over her shoulder.

My eyes grew huge, and I unashamedly picked it up and took a big bite. A delicious moan followed quickly behind, eliciting a giggle out of her. She was like Jo and had a good read on her customers.

"How are you feeling?" she asked.

I could now smile and mean it when people mentioned my pregnancy. "Thank you," I said around a mouthful of heaven. "I'm feeling well. A little queasy in the morning, but pretty much starving the rest of the day and so tired in the evening. Also, what is it with the brain fog? I swear I can't remember anything five minutes after I've heard it." I dug into my sandwich and realized everything tasted better than normal. Maybe it was my body's way of making up for everything tasting like a trashcan first thing in the morning.

"Oh, honey, pregnancy brain fog is real, but don't worry. It's not permanent." An older woman sat down at the counter beside me. "I'll have a Waldorf salad, Natalie, and an iced tea, please." The woman screamed class. She had golden blond hair in a sophisticated style above her shoulders and was chicly dressed.

"I'm Sunny Stone. I don't think we've met." I wiped my palms on a napkin and then held out my hand.

"I know who you are, my dear. Your mother talks about you all the time." She shook my hand.

I should have known my mother would be friends with a woman like this. They both were all about high society. Then I thought about the woman's words and had to force my gaping mouth closed. My mother talked about me? In a good way? I really did need to make peace with her once and for all, and not just for my sake, but for the sake of her grandchild.

"I'm Olivia Ventura," the woman continued.

"Oh, my gosh. Your husband is Antonio of Dolce Vita Stables. My husband Mitch told me all about him the other day. Mitch says he's a very nice man."

"That's my Tony." She winked but then her lips turned into a frown. "Although, he's been so stressed lately. Our horse hasn't been doing very well in the races the past month, unfortunately."

"I heard." I took a big drink of my lemonade as Natalie set Olivia's food before her, giving her a minute to take a few bites. "I hope Mark was able to help," I finally added, meaning it. Jo and Zoe seemed to think Mark was a great vet, and the stables doing well was good for the whole town.

"Mark Silverman is a godsend," Olivia replied after

dabbing the corners of her mouth. "He's worked won-
ders with our horses in the past. We were one of his
first clients when he graduated from Equine veteri-
nary school. It's hard to find a good large animal practitioner who specializes in the health management of
horses. And when you have the reputation our stables
have, it's imperative to find the best."

The bell above the café door chimed, and in
walked Rich Hastings. He took one look at me and
Olivia, then turned around and left the café. Olivia
pursed her lips and watched him through the glass
until he disappeared down the street.

Interesting.

"I take it from your expression, you don't like Rich
Hastings?" I studied her closer.

Mark had vouched for Rich, yet so far, I hadn't met
anyone else who seemed to get along with him. Plus,
he had been seen arguing with Audra Grimshaw the
first night of the Psychic Fair. I still didn't know what
that had been about, but I intended to find out.

"No, I don't much care for the man. Mark met him
years ago at the races and introduced him to Tony and
me. I always got the feeling Rich was up to no good. I
tried to warn Mark that maybe the guy wasn't a very
good influence on him, but Mark insisted he was
harmless." She shook her head. "Boys will be boys.
They never listen."

"Joanne West tried to help Rich out with his small
Finger Lakes winery because Mark asked her to, but
he didn't work out. He kept making mistakes, and she
had to fire him as her wine distributor. He didn't take
it well."

"I'm not surprised to hear he made mistakes. He
always seemed distracted and scatterbrained. As for
him not taking getting fired too well, I've seen his

temper in action. He's definitely a hothead, which was another reason I tried to warn Mark away from him, but again, it fell on deaf ears." Olivia shook her head and tsked then raised her iced tea glass high. "Cheers to only having daughters."

"Then I'm praying for a daughter," I said on a laugh.

"Oh, honey, you're a doll." She patted my hand. "I'm sure if you have a son, he will be an angel."

"Well, thank you, but speaking of boys, I should probably check in with my husband before he starts to worry."

"Ah, he's one of *those* first-time daddies."

Oh, he was one of *those* even without impending fatherhood, I thought, but said instead, "You have no idea."

IT WAS LATE AFTERNOON, AND I WAS ON MY WAY HOME. I drove past Mini Central Park and had almost made it to my house, when Morty appeared from out of nowhere. I hit the brakes and stared at him. He paced back and forth for a moment, then stood on his hind legs, pawed the air, and darted off into the woods. I wasn't worried that Morty was loose. He came and went as he pleased, but he was acting so strange lately. He seemed to be gesturing for me to follow. I pulled the car over and got out to follow him. Morty often tried to give me clues to help steer my investigation in the right direction.

I just sometimes took a while figuring out what he was trying to tell me.

It was still daylight. I should be fine venturing into the woods alone. Besides, Mitch had equipped me with pepper spray, brass knuckles, and a super bright blinding flashlight like the police use. There was probably nothing in the woods except animals anyway.

I started making my way through the woods, looking for a trail. The sun streamed through the treetops, casting rays to the forest floor. Pine needles and pinecones crunched beneath my sandals as I walked. I had a peasant skirt and blouse on with bare legs. It was summer, but the canvas of trees made the woods several degrees cooler. I shivered. Birds chirped and squirrels scurried about, but there was no sign of Morty. I was about to turn back when I heard voices. Following the sound, I crept forward, staying behind trees whenever I could.

I came to the edge of a clearing and ducked behind a tree. Peeking around the side, I saw two girls who looked to be college age, dancing about—if you could call it that—while a boy with a short ponytail and glasses took a video of them. I'd seen the dance they were attempting to do on social media, but they had a long way to go if they wanted to master it. The girls had long black hair that was pin straight and fell to their waist. I immediately knew who they were even without having met them.

The Lowenthal twins.

The question was what were they doing in the middle of the woods? This had to be what Morty was trying to show me, but why? I darted to a tree that was closer, trying to be as quiet as I could, but I wasn't the most graceful person. The boy poked his head up from the camera and searched the meadow in my direction.

"What are you doing, Danny?" one girl said with her hands on her hips.

"I thought I heard something," he replied, then

turned back to them.

"You shouldn't be paying attention to anything but us," the other girl chimed in with a hair flip.

"I've done everything you've asked of me, Ginger."

"It's not enough," she replied with a hiss. "That monster deserves everything she got after what she did to us."

"Yeah, just because she's psychic, doesn't mean she's allowed to ruin people's lives," the other twin who had to be Honey said. "I call it karma."

"I call it murder," Danny said as he looked them both in the eyes.

Ooof.

"Oh my gosh, what was that?" Ginger shrieked.

"Is it a bear?" Honey asked. "Do something, Danny!"

I stood and dusted myself off. Great, grass stains. Mitch was going to have my hide. I had been leaning so far forward, straining to hear their conversation and gauge their reactions, that my sandals slipped in the dirt and I fell flat on my face. There was no hiding I was in the woods any longer. I walked toward them and tried for a smile to put them at ease.

Their fear quickly turned to suspicion, based on their expressions.

"Who are you?" the girls asked simultaneously.

"My name is Sunny Stone. Have you seen a big, white cat? He ran off, and I was trying to find him." That much was true.

"Look, lady, we haven't seen any cat. What do you want?" Danny gripped his camera and took a step toward me.

I held up my hands. "I promise, I was just looking for my cat."

"Wait a minute. Stone is your last name? Is your

husband Detective Stone?" Ginger's eyes grew wide.

"We didn't do anything wrong." Honey moved closer to her sister and took her hand with eyes just as wide. The wind picked up and the sky grew darker with the threat of rain.

"No one is saying you did," I replied carefully. "But I couldn't help overhearing you say a woman who was psychic deserved everything that happened to her after what she did to you. Were you talking about Audra Grimshaw?"

"We didn't murder anyone," Danny blurted, trying to sound way braver than he was. The quiver in his voice gave him away. "You can't prove it." A rumble of thunder sounded off in the distance, and he looked up. "The light's no good anymore. We should go."

"Can I ask what Audra did to you?" I ignored him and looked at the girls, filling my voice with sympathy. "It must have been awful for you to dislike her so much."

"You don't have to say anything to her," Danny added, pushing his glasses back up his nose.

"No, I want to," both girls said in unison again.

"We first met Audra a year ago when she came to Syracuse University to give readings," Ginger clarified. "That's where we went to college."

"Yeah, she said we would be successful as social media influencers if we separated ourselves," Honey added. "So, we left college to pursue our dream full time. I mean, our parents are still so mad, for real."

"We spent all our college money to become the next generation of Doublemint Twins, and now we're broke," Ginger whined. "It's all her fault. She lied."

I winced, choosing my words carefully, having been through this way too many times myself. "Did you ever think maybe she meant you needed to separate from each other? The Doublemint Twins has been done. Maybe you would be more successful by coming up with something new and fresh. I'm just saying, as a psychic, people can sometimes interpret the readings we give incorrectly." The first fat raindrops began to fall. Grass stained and soaking wet. Yeah, Mitch wasn't going to be happy with me.

"I knew we couldn't trust her," Danny chimed in, obviously trying to be their hero in hopes of Lord only knew what in return. "She's one of *them*," he added. "Of course, she would stick up for what that monster did to you girls."

"I'm not sticking up for anyone. I'm just trying to get you to look at things from a different perspective. Consider all angles."

"Let's go girls." Danny stepped between them and puffed up his non-existent pecs. "I've got your backs."

Desperation to clear Sean's name filled me, and I was too impatient to wait for Mitch to call them into the station to question them, so I blurted, "You say you didn't kill her, but you did have motive to want to." The raindrops started falling harder. "That's a lot of money you went through with nothing to show for it. No college degree and no social media influencer career. I'm sure that made you pretty angry and probably a little desperate."

Honey turned around and faced me. "We *will* have something to show for it when Danny finishes fixing our videos. We have the face and body. So what if we can't dance or don't have any special skills. Danny does, and that's all that matters."

"Putting out phony content with your faces on it won't fix your problems," I tried to point out realistically.

"I already fixed their problems," Danny said.

"Really? Maybe you should talk to someone. They might go easier on you." I altered my tone from accusatory to understanding. "I mean, I could put in a good word with my husband. Let him know you're being cooperative."

"Maybe you should mind your own business," Danny added. "There's nothing for them to go easy on us for. We're innocent."

I dropped the act. "What are you getting out of this for you to be so adamant they keep quiet?"

"I don't have to tell you anything."

"Where were you girls Sunday night around eleven?" I asked, focusing my energy on the girls instead. "With motive and means, the police are going to want to know if you have an alibi."

They looked at each other with nervous expressions. "We were with Danny all night long," they said in unison.

"Ah," I looked Danny in the eye, "now I see."

"You don't see anything." He took a step toward me, lifting his camera in a threatening manner.

Lightning flashed in the sky followed by a crack of thunder too close for comfort.

Morty appeared from out of nowhere, pouncing in between Danny and myself with fangs bared and white fur glowing. They all screamed and jumped back.

"Oh, but I think I do see." I leaned down to scoop up my cat, and for once, he actually let me. "And now so do you." Morty hissed at them for good measure as I turned around and walked away, holding my breath and praying they wouldn't follow. But one thing was certain...

There was more to their story than they were letting on.

7

"**W**hat happened?" Mitch asked seconds after I walked inside of our house. He had spaghetti cooking on the stove, and it smelled amazing.

Oregano, basil, and garlic ran through my mind like whispered words of love, making my mouth water and stomach growl. I waved him off. I couldn't help it. I headed in the direction of that delicious smell before responding, intending to fill my face. I felt like I was eating for quadruplets. I didn't get two feet before he swept me off my feet.

"Oh, no you don't. You're not going anywhere until you get out of those wet clothes and warm up. And then you're going to tell me where you went."

"I can walk myself."

"Not a chance."

I sighed, settling into his big, strong arms. There was no use arguing with him, so I might as well enjoy the ride. I peeked up at his whisker covered jawline with the jagged scar peeking back at me. My wounded alpha hero had me slipping my arms around his neck and giving him the hug he obviously needed. "Are you going to be like this the whole nine months?" I asked as I rested my head on his shoulder.

I felt him shrug, but he didn't say a word.

"Then I hope we *are* having twins and I gain a ton of weight, so you can see how ridiculous you're being carrying us all." I lifted my head to see his reaction. No need. I felt his reaction through my every cell and held on tight when he missed a step and stumbled to a halt, his face paling three shades.

"Twins?" His gray eyes were cloudier than the storm raging outside.

Poor baby. I decided to have pity on him as I wiggled until he set me down. I patted his arm. "I highly doubt it's twins because we've only heard one heartbeat. I'm just having visions about twins."

He visibly relaxed. "Ah, visions, okay then."

I smirked, my pity evaporating over his non-believer tone. "Anyway, I think I know what my *visions* mean because—"

"Hold that thought," he said and pointed to our bathroom. "Shower, warm up and change. Then we'll talk over dinner."

"But—"

"I have garlic bread in the oven."

I turned around without saying a word and walked double-time to our room, listening to him chuckle as he headed back to the kitchen. The man knew the way to reach my pregnant heart. I showered and changed in record time. Ten minutes later, I emerged in the kitchen wearing yoga pants and his NYPD hoodie. It might be summer, but he was right.

I'd definitely gotten chilled in the woods for more reasons than one.

"Okay, Tink, spill it." He crossed his muscular

arms and leaned back against the counter, giving me his most intimidating stare

"I'm not afraid of you, Detective." I picked up my fork and tapped my plate. "It's gonna cost you."

His lips twitched, blowing his cover. He might be a big, tough detective, but he was a giant teddy bear on the inside. He filled both our plates, and we ate in silence. Once I was stuffed, I leaned back and groaned.

"I'm going to be as big as a house." I rubbed my barely thicker waist, imagining how much bigger it was going to get. If I was eating this much now, I was horrified to think of how much our grocery bill was going to be in my third trimester.

"You'll always be beautiful to me, babe." He reached out and squeezed my hand, his eyes full of love and sincerity.

"Awww, ditto," I replied, then realized this was as good a time as any to tell him about my grass stains. "So, about my grass stains and wet clothes...."

"I can't wait to hear this one." He grunted.

And he's back. Mr. Grumpy Pants. I grinned on the inside, loving this man more than I ever could have imagined.

His eyebrows puckered. "What's so funny."

Guess my grin hadn't been on the inside after all. "Nothing." I forced myself to stop smiling, which wasn't difficult with the thought of what I had to tell him. "I talked to Willow Goodbody like Captain Walker wanted me to the other day," I blurted. May as well just get it out. "She's staying at me parents' inn."

"I knew there was a reason you were so adamant about eating lunch there." He smiled smugly.

"Anyway, Mr. Smarty-pants, Willow definitely didn't like Audra Grimshaw. She said Audra told people she was a fake and then poached her clients."

"Sounds about right when it comes to Audra. I knew her from back when Sean dated her. You weren't here yet. I never did get a good feeling about her."

"Apparently, a lot of people felt that way. Willow said every town they go to for a Psychic Fair, Audra scouts out the people ahead of time and tries to steal them all for herself. They're supposed to be a part of the psychic community and have each other's backs, but I guess, she's the only one who's like that."

"Did you get any names of people Audra has wronged?"

"Well, she did tell me about a mental health therapist here in town. Rita Haynes. Rita doesn't believe in psychics, but I guess Audra convinced some of her clients to see her instead because she would help them more than a therapist could."

He looked me over and nodded, his lips tipping up slightly. "Nicely done, Tink."

I held my hands over my heart. "Wow, a compliment from the great detective."

"Hey, that's not really fair." He frowned. "I always give you props when you follow the rules and gain useful information during the process."

I rolled my eyes.

He ignored the gesture. "Does Willow have an alibi?"

I could feel my ears heat up. "Well, um, yes."

He arched a brow. "With whom, pray tell? Must be someone special to make you blush like that."

"Dawson Jones. She promised him a good time, and I guess he took her up on it. I'll follow up with Dawson and verify her story."

Mitch's smirk vanished. "Over my dead body. *I'll* follow up with Dawson. I don't want him anywhere near you."

"Moving on," I said, knowing I would follow up anyway. "I made an appointment for a therapy session under my maiden name."

"And she's back. My little rule breaker."

"I knew she wouldn't talk to me if I went as myself, aka the wife of Detective Mitchell Stone."

"I'm listening. May as well tell me the rest."

"It went great at first," I replied honestly, thinking about our session. "I actually learned a lot about myself and my fears for this pregnancy, with me not knowing what I'm doing and Granny Gert getting older." I rubbed my throbbing temple. "I need to make amends with my mother for good, by the way."

His lips parted. "I've been telling you that for months, but you didn't listen. I don't know why I'm surprised. You never listen to me."

"That's not true. I don't listen to unreasonable Detective Grumpy Pants, but I always listen to open minded Husband Mitch."

"My advice was not unreasonable this time."

"So, you admit it is at other times."

"I plead the fifth."

"Wise decision, Detective. Anyway, she's a therapist." I shrugged. "I figured you were crazy to think my mother and me could ever work out all our issues so why try? But maybe you had a point if a mental health therapist agrees."

I could tell he wanted to roll *his* eyes this time, but he just snapped his mouth closed and shook his head. "Continue. Reasonable Mitch is all ears."

"Good." I blew him a kiss. "Now, where was I? Oh, yeah. It didn't take her long to figure out who I was." I held up my hands. "She got so angry."

"Gee, I can't imagine why," he responded dryly.

"Maybe Reasonable Sunny can see it's understandable for someone who's been tricked to get angry."

"Good one." I clapped my hands.

"I thought so." He grinned.

"Anyway, she refused to give me an alibi, but she did let it slip that two of her clients, Ginger and Honey Lowenthal, were furious with a reading Audra gave them and vowed their revenge."

"Good." He nodded and wrote a note in his notebook. "They sound like viable persons of interest to follow up with."

"That's exactly what I thought."

His pen paused, and he looked up at me. "What did you do?"

"I didn't do anything wrong." I lifted one shoulder. "Morty suddenly appeared on the side of the road, and then he bolted into the woods. After the way he's been acting lately, I followed him."

"Of course, you did." Mitch groaned. "I'm trying not to be over protective, but you're seriously going to put me into an early grave, Sunny. You do know that, don't you?"

"You'll be fine. *I* was fine. I brought all the devices you gave me. I think I'm armed better than Inspector Gadget. Besides, I knew Morty was there if I needed him."

Mitch's eyes narrowed. "How'd you get the grass stains?"

"Patience, darling," I drawled dramatically. "I'm getting to that."

"I don't need a dissertation, just the facts, Ma'am." He mimicked Inspector Gadget's voice, but I knew he was serious.

Men.

"You're such a guy," I said, and he shrugged, unable to deny that, and actually appeared proud. I shook my head. There was no hope for his gender, so I moved on by filling him in on what the twins and Danny had said, and everything else that happened.

"So that's why Morty is here. Even *he* is worried about you. That says a lot. Maybe you should listen to him, or is he being unreasonable too?"

"For whatever reason Morty is here, I'm glad to have him around." He appeared under the table at my feet but, other than in the woods, he still wouldn't let me hold him. He kept pacing and acting unusually strange, but at least he was here.

Mitch stayed calm and relaxed, finally getting used to him. He studied Morty before saying, "I have to say I'm in agreement with that. You need two sets of eyes watching you with this latest murder and you insisting on working the case." Morty eyed my husband as if an understanding passed between them.

Good Lord, what had I done?

I didn't need both of them being over protective. I focused back on the case. "We just have to follow up with Dawson to verify Willow's alibi, then question Rita again to get answers to her whereabouts, and keep an eye on the twins and Danny to see if they slip up about their stories. I feel like they're hiding something." I jotted everything down in my notebook. "What about you? Did you find out anything? I'm really worried about Sean. We need something since he doesn't have an alibi and definitely had motive and means."

"Agreed." Mitch flipped through his notebook. "I talked to Detective Fuller, and he said many people who attended the Psychic Fair claimed to have heard the conversation Rich Hastings had when he was arguing with Audra on the first night. They said he was angry because she told everyone his wine was awful, so his was the worst seller in the beverage tent. Couple that with Jo firing him because of the mistakes Sean caught, Rich could have killed Audra after everyone left and tried to pin the blame on Sean."

"I met Olivia Ventura, by the way," I added. "Really nice lady, and she is friends with my mother which doesn't surprise me. They're both very sophisticated. Anyway, she told me she never liked Rich. That she thought he was a bad influence on Mark, but Mark wouldn't listen to her."

"Interesting." Mitch made another note in his notebook. "I haven't been able to talk to Rich yet, but I plan to find out if he has an alibi for the night of the murder."

"Good idea. Any other leads?"

"I talked to Greg Gates, Audra's boyfriend. He's still very angry about her cheating on him. At first, he was adamant that Sean was the one she cheated with because he knew she had never gotten over him. But now he's not so sure the man is Sean."

"How come? We all saw how mad and determined Greg was that the affair was with Sean. Why would he suddenly change course?"

"I'm not sure. He won't say why he's having doubts now, but I have a feeling he found something." Mitch's face turned hard. "I don't know or care about Audra, but no woman should be treated that way. Greg's not even upset that Audra was murdered. He's more concerned with his bruised ego because she cheated on him. I think he's out for revenge and wants to seek vindication himself."

"He did seem the type. He had an arrogant vibe when he ambushed Sean."

"Exactly, and he also doesn't have an alibi for after

he left the park. He says he was out all night, looking for Sean to finish their fight but never found him. Of course, he has no one who can prove that's true."

My stomach twisted into a sour knot. "We could have a second murder on our hands if he finds the real cheater."

"Divinity can't afford for that to happen." Our gazes met. "We need to step up our game. I'm looking into Audra's phone records and whereabouts from the time she arrived in Divinity leading up to her death. We need to reach the man she was cheating with before Greg for sure, or who knows what will happen."

"Sounds like a plan." Mitch's including me in the investigation by saying *we* meant more than he knew. He was finally treating me like a real partner. Now if only I could get him to truly believe in my abilities. "I'll get the girls and go to Hastings Tastings. Zoe could use a girls' day out, and maybe we'll get lucky and find Rich."

Morty walked across the kitchen floor with a piece of paper stuck to his paw. It fell off just before he left through the door. Mitch walked over and picked it up. "It's a flyer for the races coming up this weekend."

"Olivia Ventura said Mark first met Rich at the races."

"Maybe a conversation with Mark is worth revisiting. Rich blames Sean for getting him fired, and Mark blames Sean for winning Zoe's heart. Seems there are a few people who would love to see Sean take the fall for Audra's death."

"Then that's a few too many." I stood up and headed for my coat. "Come on, Detective. We have work to do."

"Tomorrow." He intercepted me and grabbed my hand. "Tonight, we're going to get to know our baby."

My heart melted.

"I read we should talk to your stomach and play music. Things like that." He shrugged. "They can hear, you know." He snagged a book from the table that I hadn't even noticed sitting there. I scanned the title, and my eyes sprang wide. It was about all the stages of pregnancy and how the baby develops. He really was going to be Superdad.

"Who are you and what have you done to my husband?"

He laughed. "Come with me and I'll show you."

Well, how could I say no to that.

8

The next morning, I pulled into the service bay of Dawson's Digs and cut the engine to my VW Bug. The sound of power tools and the smell of motor oil permeated the air through my open window. I'd never been here before. Looking around, I was impressed and happy for Dawson. His garage wasn't as big as Big Don's Auto, but he'd done well for himself. Dawson snagged a clipboard off the service station desk and headed in my direction, looking tall, dark and rugged. I'd never noticed how much he looked like Mitch. Even their walks were similar. How had I missed that?

I got out of the car.

Dawson looked up and blinked, halting in his tracks.

"Hey, Sunny. I didn't expect to see you here."

His eyes scanned my outfit, making me rethink the black and yellow sunflower sundress I'd donned. I wasn't trying to look pretty or anything, I just...I don't know. I just wanted things to be the way they used to between us.

"You look nice," he continued, then he glanced back at his clipboard.

"Thank you. I'm so sorry about the wrongful accusation of you trying to sabotage my wedding."

"No harm done." He shrugged. "Marriage agrees with you."

"Thank you, Dawson. You too." We had been friends. I hated the awkwardness between us now.

"I'm not married," he replied, meeting my eyes with a blank expression. I hated that I couldn't read what he was thinking.

"I mean, you look nice, too," I rambled. "Not that marriage agrees with you." A bubble of hysteria popped out of my mouth as a laugh before I kept rambling. "But I bet if you *were* married, it would agree with you. Not that I want you to get married, or that I don't want you to get married. I mean—"

"What can I help you with," he steered the ridiculous conversation back on track, thank goodness.

"My girl is acting up again," I gladly said in a language we both understood.

He quirked a brow. "Why didn't you bring her to Big Don's Auto?"

"They're full all day. Besides, you know her better than anyone."

"Maybe it's time you put her out of her misery."

"Bite your tongue. That's blasphemy. Would you put your grandmother out of her misery just because she's old and shakes when she moves?"

His lips twitched as we relived the same conversation we'd had for the first six months I'd been in Divinity. My car would break down. I would take her to Big Don's Auto and spend a fortune getting her fixed. Dawson would tell me it was time. I needed to put the poor girl out of her misery. I would scold him for teasing me because he knew full well I would probably go to my grave still driving this car.

He sighed dramatically, but we both knew it was fake. "I guess I can take a look. What's wrong this time?"

"What *isn't* wrong?"

"That's my point."

"Yeah yeah." I laughed, and looked him in the eye, growing serious. "It's really good talking to you again, Dawson. It's been a minute."

"It has, and I'm sorry about that." His eyes softened. "It wasn't your fault. I'm sorry for letting you think it was."

"Don't be sorry. You seriously don't have anything to be sorry for." I shook my head no, over and over. "I'm the one who's sorry for being so bad at dating."

"Clearly, you've done something right." His gaze fell to my slightly less flat stomach, and he grinned. "Congratulations, by the way."

My hands covered my bump, and I smiled with happiness. "I *have* done something right, haven't I?"

"You sure have. I really am happy for you, Sunny." His eyes and tone told me he was sincere.

"Thank you. That means a lot. What about you?" I asked. "I want you to be happy as well."

"I'm doing okay." His face flushed a little if I wasn't mistaken.

"Willow Goodbody is a beautiful woman."

The flush deepened, and he cleared his throat as he walked over to the counter. "She's a nice enough woman, but she's only here temporarily. As soon as everyone is cleared, she'll be moving on to the next Psychic Fair." He held out his hand, and I handed him the keys to my car as he filled out a form.

"Willow said she gave you a reading and then spent the night with you the evening of the murder. Is that correct?"

He eyed me curiously.

"I promise I really did need my car fixed and Big Don's *was* full today, but I thought since I'm here, I might as well verify her alibi."

He lifted a shoulder and looked up as if remembering, then nodded. "Yes, it was Sunday night. The last day of the festival. She was lonely, and I was lonely. The rest is history. Nothing more complicated than that."

"Have you seen her since?"

"Around town, but she hasn't been back to my place if that's what you're asking." He set his pen back on the counter.

"I'm sorry it didn't work out for you. Hopefully, you'll find someone amazing because you deserve it."

"It's okay, Sunny. My ego was a little bruised back then, but I'm fine. Seriously." He smiled a genuine smile.

I smiled back and then started to head for the door when he asked, "What time did they estimate the murder happened?"

"Between eleven p.m. and twelve a.m., why?"

He hesitated for a moment as if torn, but then finally answered, "I like Willow, but Sean is my friend. Willow Goodbody didn't get to my place until nearly one a.m. I have no clue what she was doing before that."

"Well, this is certainly an interesting turn of events," I said.

"Why, yes, it is," came a deep rumbling voice from behind me. "It certainly is."

I didn't have to be psychic to know I was busted.

"Well, I'm officially in the doghouse," I said to Jo and Zoe at Papas' Greek restaurant. "I hadn't expected to be here so soon after the honeymoon."

The smells of various meats, greens, and olives assaulted my senses with delight while the clatter of silverware against plates and the hum of conversation filled the background. Marble pillars and statues were scattered about, making customers feel as if they were actually in ancient Greece.

Nikko's Italian restaurant with old school Italy decor was just down the street, and the owners were often trying to outdo each other. I paid equal homage to both. Dawson's garage was just down the street from the local restaurants. I'd walked there, all too happy to get away from my fuming detective husband, and called the girls on the way, asking them to meet me for lunch.

"Spill the tea, girl." Jo rubbed her hands together. "I need to talk about something other than diaper rash cures and when to start oatmeal."

"Well, my car was having problems, so I brought it to Dawson's garage to be fixed." I couldn't quite meet their eyes.

"Oh, boy," Zoe said.

"Oh, yeah," I replied, looking up and feeling my cheeks warm.

"Why not Big Don's Autobody?" Jo eyed me curiously.

"I was going to take it there, but Belle said they were booked full for today." I waved my hands in front of my face. "That is the truth, I swear." I dropped my hands and wrinkled my nose. "Could it have waited a day? Yes, but I saw this as my opportunity to clear the air with Dawson." I blew out a big breath. "What a mess this has turned out to be. He used to be my friend, and it's been so awkward between us ever since I accidentally shot him down when he was trying to ask me out."

"I hate to be the voice of reason, but you've had all sorts of time to clear the air," Zoe asked. "Why now?"

"Willow Goodbody claims she spent the night with Dawson the evening of the murder. One of us had to verify her story."

"Then what's the problem?" Jo took a bite of her Caesar salad. She told us she was trying to lose weight after having the twins, which was crazy if you asked me. She looked amazing, especially with nursing the two human garbage disposals who seemed to have bottomless pits for stomachs. "Earth to Sunny. Where'd you go?"

"Sorry. My mind is a mess these days." I refocused on our conversation. "Dawson and I really did clear the air, and we're fine now. I feel so much better about that, but I knew Mitch would be angry. He specifically said he would handle talking to Dawson."

"Ohhh." Jo wiped her mouth with a napkin.

"Yeah." I shoved a gyro in mine.

"Men can be so touchy," Zoe said, pushing the fluffy layer of bechamel sauce and cheese around the top of her moussaka, not eating a bite. "Lately, Sean takes everything I say to him the wrong way."

"He's just stressed about being a suspect and not being able to do anything about it." Jo sipped her water. "Remember how bad Cole was?"

"Mitch too," I agreed, sipping my milk. "It's so silly, though. I'm married to him, not Dawson. In fact, I didn't even date Dawson. My car needed fixing, I made amends with a friend, and I got what I needed for the case. Willow didn't actually show up until after the estimated time of death for Audra, so her story has holes in it now. If Mitch had been the one to talk to Dawson, he may not have given him anything on Willow. I will do whatever it takes to clear Sean's name, even if it means sitting in the doghouse."

"And I appreciate that more than you know." Zoe fidgeted with her napkin. "I don't know what I'll do if Sean goes to jail for murder."

"He won't, and that's that." I took her hand and tried to let my energy flow into her. "I can feel it."

Her eyes met mine and filled with hope. "You really think so?"

I needed to give her something to hang on to. "What are you ladies doing for the rest of the afternoon?" I asked with a mischievous grin.

"Honey, I cleared my day when you called," Jo said. "I could use a girls' day out, no matter where it is." Good thing because she wasn't going to like what I had to say, but it was essential, and Zoe needed this.

"I'm free," Zoe chimed in. "The only wedding I'm planning is my own, and that is on hold at the moment."

"Good, it's settled then." I set my napkin down and nodded once. "Put on a nice outfit, and let's go on a little adventure."

"Where to?" Jo eyed me cautiously.

"Finger Lakes wine country."

"Sylvia Meadows Stone, don't you know alcohol is bad for the baby," my mother said from behind me.

I turned around to see the great Vivian Meadows, Granny Gert, Great-Grandma Tootsie, and Fiona being seated at a table right by ours. How had I missed them when I came in? This pregnancy brain fog was no joke.

"I know that mother." I kept my calm, remembering the therapist's advice, before she knew who I was and threw me out of her office, that is. "That's why I'll be the DD." I smiled a little too brightly.

"DD?" Toots asked. "You kids and your lingo. I can't keep up."

"Designated Driver," I clarified.

"We can't all fit into that tiny beetle of yours," Fiona added.

"It's a Volkswagen Bug, not a beetle." I laughed, but my chuckles quickly faded as her words sank in. "Who said anything about we?"

"I think it would be okay," Zoe said. "The more the merrier."

"Well, tweedled dee dee, I have a big ole Cadillac that's just sitting at the inn. I can drive," Granny Gert chimed in.

"No!" we all said at once.

"You can drive Cole's minivan," Jo offered. She'd refused to give up her truck after the twins were born, so Cole surprised her by trading in his for a minivan. He'd earned big points for that one.

"Boys oh day, we're going on a road trip." Toots clapped her hands and hummed show tunes, swaying back and forth as her mind wandered off in thought before she added, "I haven't been on a road trip in years."

"Oh, my word, we're going to have a grand ole time." Granny Gert twittered. "I'll bake us some cookies for the road."

"And pie," Fiona chimed in. "Don't forget about my pie. Oh, this is going to be so much fun. I feel like a spring chicken." She smoothed her bottle-blond hair.

"You're all something, all right, and you're not going anywhere without me." My mother pursed her lips before adding, "I've got my eye on all of you." She looked at me and pointed. "Especially you."

How had my day gone from a girls' trip with my best friends to babysitting the Tasty Trio and listening to Mimizilla lecture me every step of the way. My mother refused to be called grandma anything and mama was reserved for me, so she'd chosen Mimi. I'd just gotten a taste of what Mimi was going to be like as a grandmother. I groaned, wishing I were anywhere but here.

Suddenly the doghouse didn't look so bad.

9

Hastings Tastings was a Finger Lakes winery situated along Seneca Lake about an hour and a half west of Divinity. It was small but quaint. With only one tasting counter, there wasn't a lot of room in the building. The rest of the space was filled with bottles of wine, glasses, magnets and other paraphernalia. Rich could use some help in arranging his winery shop, and maybe hire someone who was more organized when it came to distributing his wine. He had the right idea; he was just too green.

"I feel bad I had to let Rich go," Jo said, searching the room yet again. We'd been there for an hour already. "You owe me for being here." She sampled a chardonnay and wrinkled her nose, dumping the rest out. "Audra was right. This is awful. I hadn't tasted all of Rich's wine. The Riesling wasn't bad, but then again, the Finger Lakes region is known for producing outstanding Rieslings. I was going off Mark's recommendation. Lesson learned. Act like a businesswoman before a friend. The pinot grigio is okay but the reds are the worst." She shuddered.

"I wouldn't know about the wines, but I saw it as an opportunity to question him," I responded. "You can relax. I've looked everywhere, but I haven't seen him."

"I don't feel bad for him," Zoe said, joining us. "He obviously has an issue with anger. He got into an argument with Audra, and then he threatened Sean. I don't understand how Mark ever became friends with him in the first place, but why stay friends after he witnessed Rich's bad behavior? That's not like the Mark I knew." Zoe was the wine lover among us all. She'd taken one sip of a Sauvignon Blanc and had refused to taste any more.

I didn't blame her. I took a sip of my water. I couldn't drink any wine because of the baby, but that didn't mean my stomach wasn't turning over the overwhelming smells of the different types of wines blending together.

"The coroner did say there were signs of a struggle on Audra's body," I said, focusing on the investigation. "It makes me wonder if Rich went back to see Audra. The argument could have escalated, resulting in a struggle. He could have seen an opportunity and pushed her into the electrified puddle."

"Or she could have stumbled and fallen into the puddle," Jo said.

"Either way, Rich Hastings had the means and the motive." I set my glass down and ate a cracker. "The question is does he have an alibi?"

"Do, re, mi...mimimimimeeeee...fa, so, la, ti, do!" came a woman's operatic soprano voice from the end of the tasting counter.

"Wait, is that...?" I couldn't finish my sentence because that would be utterly ridiculous. Impossible. Never happen.

"Mimi, hahaha. Get it? That's meeeee," the voice trilled again.

I stepped away from the counter and leaned back to look down the bar. "Oh, good Lord." Several patrons had already whipped out their phones and pressed record.

"No way." Jo choked on another taste of awfulness.

"Is that your mother," Zoe asked.

"No, that's Mimi, my unborn child's future grandmother." I couldn't help but laugh a little. "And here she was worried the Tasty Trio was going to misbehave. Or worse, *me*. She's going to die when she sees this later."

Great-Grandma Tootsie hummed along, lifting her wine glass in salute as she swayed back and forth. She was more of a rye and ginger type woman, but she appeared to like the taste of Hastings wine just fine. Or maybe her taste buds weren't what they used to be as she approached a century of living.

Granny Gert waved her wooden spoon—yes, she carried it with her everywhere—around as if she were a maestro, directing a choir of one.

Fiona danced in circles, not to be outdone, clapping her hands and singing the background chorus with a few yodels thrown in.

"Ma'am?" The wine steward, called a sommelier, was a woman, and she didn't seem too happy as she flagged my attention with a towel. "Can you get the rest of your party to quiet down please? No one can hear me describe the notes and body of the wines. Or possibly get them to leave. There are others waiting to taste, and those ladies appear to have tasted every bottle we make...twice."

"I'm so sorry," I said and meant it, wincing when another rendition of operatic mimi's rang through the air, nearly shattering the glasses. "I was just waiting to meet the owner, Rich Hastings, before we left."

My eyes sprang wide. *Was that a kazoo?*

I peeked over and cringed. Sure enough, Fiona had pulled out her kazoo and Great-Grandma Tootsie was blowing into a harmonica, while Granny Gert tried to play the spoons on her thigh with her one wooden spoon.

The sommelier leveled me with a frustrated look. "Mr. Hastings has already left for the horse races in Saratoga Springs. He won't be back until the end of the week. Now, please, gather your party and leave."

"Absolutely." Interesting tidbit, considering no one was supposed to leave town until they were cleared. Last I checked, he hadn't been cleared.

Jo and Zoe had already made their way over to the circus act, while I made a mental note to add horse racing to my calendar, and make a little wager of my own.

I bet I would find the answers I was looking for at the track.

————

AFTER WE GOT HOME, MY MOTHER TOOK TWO ASPIRIN and went straight to bed.

We made plans to attend the horse races, but they weren't until the weekend, so the next day I decided Sean could use a meditation session. He was one of my best friends. I knew he was struggling with being accused of murder and the strain it put on his relationship with Zoe. I just wanted to help.

Parting the strands of crystal beads I used as a door, we entered the room I'd set aside specifically for my fortune-teller business.

My sanctuary.

It was a small, cozy room. I'd painted the walls a

soft, pale blue meant to relax the seeker while the seer
—that would be me—read his or her fortune. New age
music poured quietly out of the speakers, a tropical
fish tank bubbled away in one corner, a fireplace sat
unlit in the other corner, and various green plants and
herbs were scattered about. Constellations covered the
ceiling in a dazzling imitation of the universe, and
when I dimmed the lights, they glowed. Last but not
least, my fortune teller supplies sat on shelves in the
other corner.

An old-fashioned tea table sat in the center of one
half of the room. In the other half, I had placed yoga
mats on the floor. I walked past the table and gestured
to the mats.

"Have a seat, Sean. Make yourself comfortable."

"Okay, lass. If you think this will help, I'll try anything." He wore gym shorts with a wrinkled green
shamrock t-shirt. Running a hand through his messy
blond hair, he smiled at me but his dimples were less
deep than normal and his blue eyes had dark shadows
beneath them as if he hadn't slept in days.

"It will definitely help." I sat down across from him
on my own yoga mat. "How are you, really?"

"Not good. I just don't understand how any of this
could have happened. Audra and I were history. I
hadn't seen her in years, and then she shows up to
ruin my life right after I'm finally happy. I'm worried
Zoe will call off the wedding. She's the best thing that's
ever happened to me, but I don't know if she fully believes me."

"It didn't help when Greg Gates stormed in,
claiming you were having an affair with Audra." I
chewed my lip, thinking about the case. "Where do
you think he got the idea that you were the one
cheating with his girlfriend?"

"I honestly don't know. Audra is the one who cheated on me years ago, so I called off our engagement." He scrubbed a hand through his mess of curls and then shrugged. "Maybe she told him she was having the affair with me to get back at me, or maybe she was jealous of my happiness with Zoe. I have no clue, but she succeeded in ruining my life once more."

"That gives you a pretty strong motive."

His gaze shot to mine. "Please tell me you don't think I murdered Audra."

"Of course not. Your friends all know you're a lover not a fighter. Unfortunately, that's not enough proof for everyone else. And your life is not ruined yet." I squared my shoulders and added, "Mitch and I will do everything in our power not to let that happen. I hope *you* know that."

"I do." He nodded. "What can I do to help?"

"Try to think of anything at all that might clear your name."

He groaned. "Everything looks so bad. After Greg and I fought and Zoe stormed off, I did go back and warn Audra to stay away from us or else. It was just my frustration making me say stupid things. I wouldn't have done anything to harm anyone. I tried calling Zoe, but she wouldn't answer me. Then she texts me not to come home to our apartment. So, I turned off my phone. I couldn't handle having her say anything else to me. Then I stopped by Gretta's Grocery, bought a twelve pack, and drove to an old road on the outskirts of town to drown my sorrows and pass out. I didn't know anything bad had happened until I came back into town the next day."

"What about in the past when you and Audra were still together? Can you think of anyone else who might have had a reason to want her gone?"

He looked off, deep in thought for a moment, then he sighed. "I don't know. That was so long ago."

"Let's meditate. Maybe that will jar something."

"Okay. What do I do?"

"We'll sit in a traditional Sukhasana pose. This is the easiest yoga pose for meditation. Cross your legs with your feet beneath your knees. Keep your spine and neck straight, with your chin slightly raised, and try to relax."

"Like this?" Sean did as I told him.

"Yes, that looks great. Next, we'll focus on our hand positions, called the mudra. Mudra is about connecting your chakras, aligning your sensory receptors and creating a deep connection with your mind, body, and spirit. The type of position you use will determine the flow of energy you receive throughout your body."

"If you say so." He laughed, looking skeptical.

I loved these teaching moments of my job. "For example, the way you hold your hands influences the way you hold your mind." I gave him a nod as I could already feel the energy in our small space shift.

"I don't really understand any of it, but I'm game to try." He shook out his hands, in a ready position.

"Just keep an open mind. Many people underestimate how important the hand position is for meditation. There are hundreds of mudras to choose from, but I think in your case, we should focus on the Chin Mudra."

"I thought we were talking about our hands?" His features pinched with confusion.

"We are." I smiled in reassurance. "The name Chin doesn't have anything to do with the chin on your face. It has to do with the consciousness seal. His brows raised as if I'd sprouted horns, and I couldn't suppress the giggle. "It has to do with stimulating the root chakra, which further deepens your connection to the earth." I paused to make sure I hadn't lost him, then demonstrated what I wanted him to do. "Touch your index finger to your thumb, forming a circle or seal. Straighten your other fingers, then turn your hands over so your palms are facing down and place them over your knees." Sean did as I directed, while I watched.

"Close your eyes, relax and breathe. Empty your mind of thoughts and clear your head." I could see him begin to relax after several moments. "Can you feel the sense of grounding and humbling energies?" I asked.

"Actually, yes. That's amazing."

"Now, keeping your eyes closed and your mind cleared, let's focus on your mindful breathing. Breathe in through your nose for four seconds, then hold your beath for seven seconds before finally exhaling through the mouth for eight seconds. This will help manage anxiety and you should sleep better at night. Repeat it four times when you're anxious or can't sleep."

After several more rounds of breathing, Sean opened his eyes. "I'm feeling a difference already. Thank you, Sunny. I really appreciate it."

"There are so many other techniques in meditation. We can always explore them if you want. I think this is a good start, though." Sean was a great student, but I could sense he was still troubled.

"What happens if I get distracted when trying to meditate?"

"Distractions are normal. Don't beat yourself up about it, and don't force your mind to refocus. Acknowledge what distracted you, then ease yourself back into the meditation. The more you practice, the more meditating will become comfortable and a healthy habit."

"I'll try." He looked at me with a mixture of worry and sadness. "Sunny, do you think Zoe will leave me?"

"Oh, Sean, I'm so sorry you're going through this. No, I don't think Zoe will leave you. She loves you and believes in you. I know this for a fact, but it's been a lot for her, too. The truth will come out. It always does."

"I hope you're right. I don't want to lose her." He sounded so defeated; my heart ached for him.

"Let's practice your breathing together." I reached out and took his hands in mine, hoping to bring his mind to a better place. "Now, close your eyes, relax your mind and body, and just breathe."

Sean slowly began to relax. I could feel his energy, feel the tension begin to leave his body. I slowed my own breathing and focused.

My eyes drifted into tunnel vision, the world fading away just like it always did when I was pulled into a vision. I was in Audra's body, walking hand-in-hand with Sean along Main Street. The love he felt was evident in the way he looked at her. They shopped together and vacationed together and dined in restaurants together. All the fancy things Audra liked to do, they did. I didn't see them do any of the adventurous outdoor things he and Zoe liked to do. I definitely sensed the relationship was one-sided, with her doing all the taking and no giving. I felt her arousal and passion for him, but I didn't feel love.

Time moved forward, and I finally felt a love so strong, it made her giddy. Her passion was deeper than ever to the point where I could feel her obsession with him. I saw Sean propose to her, and she said yes. Time went by and her love grew. I couldn't help wonder what went wrong between them because they'd obviously been in love.

Suddenly, she was hiding behind some bushes in the park. I could feel the thrill she felt over keeping this secret. Why would she need to keep a secret with Sean? They stepped out from behind the bushes into the light, and I gasped.

The man wasn't Sean.

"Sunny, are you okay?" Sean asked, yanking me back to the present.

I let go of his hands and inhaled a shaky breath. "I saw it all. Your whole relationship with Audra. I'm so sorry. It was clear you loved her, but she never did love you. I think she liked the idea of you, but she always had bigger aspirations."

He nodded, his face looking disgusted. "Yup, I knew she was cheating on me. She was late a lot and always on her phone. I heard her talking to him once and telling him she loved him and why couldn't they be together. That she wanted more than just an affair. I confronted her about it, but she refused to tell me who she was having the affair with. So, I broke things off with her. I'm sure he never gave her anything more because she moved away shortly after and hasn't been back."

"You're right. He didn't give her anything more," my gaze held Sean's captive as I finished with, "because he was married."

His eyes widened. "How do you know?"

"I saw him."

His jaw hardened. "Who was it?"

"Councilman Michael McMasters, who's married to the head of the ladies Auxiliary club, Beth Mc-Masters."

"But he's like fifty." Sean scowled. "Audra always did like older men."

"I'm pretty sure she liked his money and clout, too. I'm also almost positive he is the man she was having an affair with again this time."

"I wonder if Greg knows?" Sean speculated. "That's probably why he backed off from me. What does this mean for the case?"

"This means, my friend, we have a new suspect."

10

The weekend was here, and I had to admit, excitement trickled down my spine. Saratoga Race Course was a thoroughbred race track that had been around since eighteen sixty-three. Horses raced from mid-July through Labor Day in September. The Travers Stakes was the most popular day of the summer racing season, kind of like New York's Derby Day. I had never been to a race but had always wanted to go. This case gave us the perfect opportunity.

Saratoga was about two and a half hours from Divinity. The gates opened at eleven and the first race started around one. We paid for grandstand seats, but many horse owners sat in the clubhouse in their own section. I was pretty sure that was where Dolce Vita Stables owners, Antonio and Olivia Ventura, were sitting. I didn't see my parents yet, but knowing my mother, she and my father had probably scored an invite into their suite.

"This is fun," Jo said. "It's nice to get out of Divinity for a while, with everything that's going on."

"Agreed," I said. "I wish Zoe and Sean could have come with us."

"Me too, but then I wouldn't have had a babysitter."

"True."

"I just love those crazy ladies." Jo pointed a little ways away from our seats, and I couldn't help but giggle.

Mitch and I had ridden with Cole and Jo. Zoe and Sean stayed behind because Sean hadn't been cleared as a suspect. Great-Grandma Tootsie, Granny Gert, Fiona, Harry, and Captain Walker all rode together. The Trio all wore spring dresses and shoes that matched the most outlandish hats, while their dates wore pastel-colored suits and bowties. Even Morty had magically appeared at the racetrack as they arrived, sporting a new bowtie, but he had disappeared into the stables moments later. Morty did as he wished and would find his way back to them when he was ready. Meanwhile, I tried to tell them all this wasn't the Kentucky Derby, but they didn't care.

"They certainly know how to make an impression," I said.

"Speaking of impressions, has your mother recovered from being center stage?" Jo sipped a hard seltzer.

My father wanted to dress like the other men, but my mother was having none of that, bringing their high society outfits out of retirement from their New York City days. She wasn't taking any chances of an outlandish repeat of the winery, keeping Vivian firmly in charge so Mimi wouldn't emerge again and steal the show. Standing out was the last thing on her mind after her last performance, but no matter what she did to keep it quiet, the word had spread faster than her vibrato had trilled that day.

Mortified wasn't strong enough of a word for how she felt.

"I personally enjoyed seeing her loosen up for once," I responded, "but I doubt we'll see a repeat occurrence anytime soon." Scanning the crowd, I looked for Rich Hastings, but still didn't see him.

There were three tracks at the race course. A main dirt track and two turf tracks, ranging in different distances depending on the race. A gazebo that was part of the Saratoga Race Track logo was a permanent fixture on the infield. I'd spotted Mark Silverman near the training track, talking to the jockey who would ride Sweet Life in today's race, but we were too far away to talk to Mark yet. I was hoping he would know if Rich was here.

I sipped my water we'd gotten from the mineral spring called the Big Red in the picnic grounds earlier. This was the mineral water that made Saratoga Springs famous. Meanwhile, the Trio and their beaus were sipping Mint Juleps.

Mitch and Cole joined Jo and me after placing their bets.

"Did you see any signs of Rich?" I asked. I'd told him what I'd heard at the winery, and we were here to follow up.

"Not yet. I thought maybe we'd catch him placing a bet. Then again, he could have placed some off-track bets. He's been laying low since the murder. I haven't been able to track down Greg Gates, either."

I had told Mitch about my vision during my meditation session with Sean. He said he would look into Councilman McMasters and his wife, but that was tricky since the only proof I had of anything was in my mind. Getting ahold of Greg was the key. I had a hunch he'd found something out, otherwise he never would have stopped harassing Sean.

The sound of a bell pierced the air, and the hum of

excitement filtered through the crowd as the jockeys were called to the paddock. The path from the stables to the paddock ran through the picnic grounds so spectators could have a close-up view of the horses being walked out and saddled before entering the chutes. Mark checked Sweet Life over one more time before handing the reins to the jockey. The iconic bugle call sounded, and the jockeys walked off with the horses to the chutes. The race would start in ten minutes.

I was about to turn away when I saw Rich Hastings off to the side. He motioned for Mark to join him in the shadows. They stood with their heads bent together, the conversation looking intense. Rich finally walked off. Mark looked around and waited a minute before he walked away in the other direction. I was about to make an excuse about needing a bathroom break, but the announcer came on the speakers stating the race was about to start and final bets must be placed.

A few minutes later, the chute doors sprang open, and the horses charged out of their chutes. They barreled around the track at breakneck speeds. The crowd went wild, calling out their favorites and cheering the jockeys on. We all got caught up in the action, cheering for Sweet Life. He was in fourth place but had picked up speed, overtaking third. When he rounded the corner and claimed the second spot, I jumped up and down, screaming his name. Mitch chuckled beside me, but shouted his own encouragement. Jo was even louder than I was, and Cole's voice boomed over everyone's.

I had a moment of worry over the Trio and their entourage. What if one of them had a heart attack? The final stretch pulled my thoughts back to the race.

Sweet Life was closing in on the number one spot with only seconds to go. They crossed the finish line, and the crowd grew quiet. It wasn't clear who had won. After a few moments of viewing the photo finish, the announcer came over the speakers.

"Devil's Fury wins by a nose!"

Half the crowd cheered and the other half booed. Sweet Life had been favored to win, but this was the third race in a row he'd lost by a nose. The next race would start in twenty minutes, so we made our way down to the winner's circle and looked around. Mark and Rich were nowhere to be seen, but Antonio Ventura stood by his jockey and Sweet Life, talking intensely and looking frustrated.

Meanwhile, Olivia and my parents headed our way after spotting us. Antonio caught up with them after his jockey led Sweet Life back to the stables. The Trio and their beaus found us and even Morty had returned, riding in Great-Grandma Tootsie's arms, but looking restless.

"That was so close," Mitch said to Antonio.

"Close won't keep my stables going, unfortunately." Antonio sounded discouraged, his shoulders slumping in defeat.

"It's okay, Tony." Olivia rubbed his back. "He'll win the next race."

"That's what you said the last time." He stepped forward until her arm fell away, then he massaged the back of his neck. The strain on his face was evident, and the gray in his hair more pronounced. "We can't afford any more losses."

"What does Mark have to say?" I asked.

Antonio's expression pinched. "He can't find anything wrong with him. I don't know what more to do. Something has to change for us to stay in business."

"But your reputation is huge," Jo said. "You must have other horses in the races and retired horses with stud fees to help out."

"Not when bad investments put a dent in my profits," Antonio muttered. "Do you have a minute to—"

Olivia quickly jumped in with, "Oh, nothing's as bad as that." She glanced at her watch. "Would you look at the time? We have other engagements we must attend to. I'm sure you all understand." She turned to my parents. "Thank you for joining us, Vivian and Donald. It was a pleasure hosting you." She looped her arm through Antonio's and led him away, post haste. By the stiffness of her shoulders, she was none too happy with him. That didn't surprise me. She was just like my mother. All about appearances.

And it appeared Dolce Vita Stables wasn't as well off as everyone thought.

THE NEXT MORNING, I WAS SHOPPING AT GRETTA'S Grocery. I had to stop eating out so much and attempt to learn how to cook. I wasn't even that far along, and I already had to undo the top button of my shorts. Besides, what kind of mother would I be if I didn't know how to cook? That made me think of my own mother. She didn't raise me on takeout, but we did dine in fine restaurants frequently. And when we ate at home, we had a personal chef, a butler, a maid and a nanny.

Not exactly a warm and fuzzy household.

I smiled, thinking of my grandmother. Granny Gert was about as warm and fuzzy as they came. I would stay with her a lot because it felt like home. She prepared home-cooked meals with my favorite dessert, of course. Cookies! And tucked me in at night.

That was the type of house I wanted for my child.

Nodding my head once, I inhaled a deep breath and grabbed a shopping cart, waving to Gretta as I passed by her office. A lot of Divinity's businesses chose to go with a theme when decorating. Many chose historical themes from Italy, Greece, and even the West. Gretta, however, had chosen flower power as her theme. Her floor was green, with yellow walls and flowers stenciled everywhere to the point of making one's head spin.

I could do this, I thought, inhaling a cleansing breath and ignoring the dizzying decor. I didn't have to be like my mother. I could be any type of mother I wanted. And maybe my mother would turn out to be a better grandmother—er Mimi. I still had to have a talk with her and let her know how I had felt for years, and that I forgave her. Maybe then we could finally move forward into the relationship I had always dreamed about.

I looked at my list and gasped. It was twice as long as the original one I had created last night. Mitch had added all sorts of things that were not on the outside perimeter of the store, aka the healthy section according to Gretta. Oh no, Mitch's items were on the aisles in the center next to all the candy, cookies and chips. Grumpy Pants got hangry if he didn't have his treats, yet he expected me to eat healthy because of the baby. How was that fair? I shook my head.

I gathered all of the items on the outside section of the store, and then in a moment of weakness, I turned to the inside aisles. Maybe we could compromise and just get a few goodies, but if he thought he would be the only one eating them, he had another think coming. The store wasn't busy this morning. I waved at a few of the Sewing Sisters and Knitting Nanas, but those were the only people I saw. My shopping was moving along quite nicely, and I didn't feel like half as much an imposter as I thought I would.

I was picking up the marshmallow cereal my husband had on the list, when I heard voices raise on the other side of the aisle. It sounded like two men. I couldn't hear well enough, so I quietly made my way down the cereal aisle and moved to the end of the row, pretending to study the breakfast items on the endcap. I leaned to the side ever so slightly and peeked around the corner and blinked.

Greg Gates was standing across from Michael Mc-Masters, their shopping carts squaring off as if they were about to duel. I didn't know what Greg Gates did for a living because he didn't live in Divinity, but I knew Michael McMasters was the head of the Town Council and a highly respected member of the community.

"You're not going to get away with this," Greg said and clenched his fists over the bar of his cart.

Michael backed up a step and raised his hands up from his own cart in a non-threatening way. "I'm sorry, but I don't know what you're talking about."

"I'm not buying that for a second." Greg rolled his cart forward a couple inches. "You used Audra years ago when she was engaged to Sean O'Malley. She begged you for more than just an affair, but you coldly refused."

"You can't prove a thing." Michael stiffened his spine and adjusted his tie. "I'm married and have a child. Why would I jeopardize that?"

"Because you're a man of power. You love the attention it brings you, and the women who come along with that. You're old, and Audra was beautiful. You didn't deserve her. After you were through with her, you abandoned her, so she left Divinity." Greg leaned forward and growled, "That's when she met me."

"I'm not admitting to anything," Michael replied like a true politician, "but even if I were to admit to this nonsense, that was years ago. Why bring it up now? Like you said, she moved on with you."

"The Psychic Fair wasn't the first time Audra came back to Divinity. She came back a few months ago, and when she returned, she grew distant from me. We started having problems, and she pushed me away. I knew something had happened in Divinity, but she wouldn't tell me the truth."

"That has nothing to do with me. I heard you thought she had an affair with Sean O'Malley. Why don't you harass him instead of bothering an innocent man?"

"I did." Greg laughed harshly. "Funny how it turns out that he's the innocent man, and you're the lying loser."

"You might want to check yourself and remember who you're talking to." Michael regripped his cart and hardened his jaw. "I have connections."

"So do I." Greg gave him an evil grin. "Only *my* friends don't wear suits and don't much care if they get arrested."

"Alright, you say you have proof that I was the one Audra had the affair with again this time around." Michael eyed him closely. "So, show me your proof. Otherwise, I'll sue you for slander."

"I'm not stupid, pal. The proof is hidden for safe-keeping, but I'll tell you what it is. Audra had a diary. When I couldn't find Sean the night of her murder, I went back to our hotel and found her diary hidden in a secret compartment of her suitcase. It made for some very interesting reading that night." Greg paused.

Michael paled, but he didn't say anything.

Greg continued, "Like I said, Audra came back a few months ago, and you decided to use her all over again. Only this time, she'd learned a thing or two over the years. She learned how to get what she wanted this time around."

"And what would that be?"

"What's she's always wanted. For you to leave your wife and marry her."

Michael laughed humorlessly, looking down his nose. "That would never happen. I have a child to think about."

"Yes, you do...or did, anyway." Greg bumped Michael's cart hard until he stumbled back a step. "Audra was pregnant and says it's yours."

Michael's jaw unhinged.

"That's right, you jerk," Greg growled. "We hadn't been together in months, so it definitely wasn't mine. She planned to tell you the last night of the fair."

Michael started shaking his head no.

Greg bumped him hard again until he stumbled. "I'm thinking she *did* tell you, and you murdered them both."

I gasped and jerked, sending breakfast bars and oatmeal flying. Two startled sets of eyes locked with mine.

"Cleanup in Aisle 10," came over the loud speaker.

Something told me it would take more than a broom and dustpan to clean up this mess.

11

I still couldn't wrap my head around Audra Grimshaw being pregnant with Michael McMaster's baby. I had to know if his wife knew anything about it.

On Sunday afternoon, I paid a visit to Divinity's library with my best friend Jo. I remembered the first time I'd stepped foot in the library when I first moved to Divinity, thinking it was smaller than I'd thought it would be. Scenic pictures of the Adirondack Mountains and rivers of upstate New York graced the walls. Light oak bookshelves stood in rows like a set of dominoes, and small tables were scattered about in strategic places.

It was pleasant and inviting.

"Follow me," Jo said, as we walked through the front doors.

As we made our way to the back of the library, we saw Olivia Ventura sitting at a table behind several large, leather-bound books. She raised her head and smiled back as we waved. Mother had said the woman was the self-appointed historian for the Ventura family. One of her many hobbies.

There was a large meeting room in the back reserved for several organizations. The National Ladies Auxiliary Sons of the American Revolution, was holding a monthly meeting this particular Sunday. It was open for the public to observe in the interest of joining, but once the meeting started, all non-members had to leave.

The library was situated between City Hall in one direction, and the American Legion in the other, across the street from Warm Beginnings and Cozy Endings Cafe. Beth McMasters, wife of Councilman Michael McMasters, was the head of the Ladies Auxiliary. The group consisted of women related by marriage to members in good standing, or bloodline to members in good standing, or members deceased while in good standing of the NSSAR.

My Grandpa Frank fought in several wars, and Granny Gert used to be a member of the Ladies Auxiliary before it became too much for her. I qualified for Ladies Auxiliary for both the American Legion or the Sons of the American Revolution.

My mother had never shown much of an interest in joining, but she had fought for truth and justice and the American way quite successfully for more than half of her life. I might be interested in joining, but I was definitely interested in talking to Beth McMasters. Jo was one of eight children and was already a member, having come from a long line of military families. We sat in the back and observed.

The organization had been of major assistance to the National Society by raising thousands of dollars to help the Society in carrying out its mission of inspiring patriotism and informing others of the contributions of our revolutionary ancestors. They held many social and fundraising events to support the

SAR programs with their objectives to advance America's Heritage.

Jo's brothers and father were also members of the American Legion, the nation's largest wartime veterans service organization aimed at advocating patriotism across the U.S. through diverse programs and member benefits.

With a rap of the gavel, the meeting was called to order and any non-members were asked to leave. I found the treasurer and handed in my application form. I'd still have to wait until after the investigative committee confirmed I qualified for membership and if they would vote to let me in... This was an organization I could truthfully get behind and had been thinking about for a while, but now more than ever, I was compelled to join.

Truth and justice for all, but especially Sean O'Malley.

I sat outside the room in awe, able to hear every word.

Beth McMasters instructed the secretary to call the roll of Officers. After three raps, Beth said, "Color Bearers, secure and present to colors." And the meeting was underway.

It was very clear that Beth enjoyed the power, as periodically during the meeting her voice was loud and commanding through the wall. At times it sounded like she was ordering them through some kind of formation. Even with my gift of site, I couldn't figure out exactly what they were doing. But I became even more eager to be a full-fledged member, something that would connect me even more to the community of Divinity which I loved so much.

But first, I needed to have some face-to-face time with Beth McMaster.

I heard the members recite the Pledge of Allegiance and then break into song with the National Anthem. Beth gave three raps of the gavel. "I now declare this Auxiliary meeting open for the transaction of such business as may properly come before it."

I listened while they discussed new member admissions. Then they went over the minutes from the previous meeting and any corrections. Next up was the treasurer's report and presentation of bills. Reports from the committees were covered next, followed by unfinished business and new business. Lastly, they covered the reports from the trustees, followed by suggestions for the good of the order.

Beth said, "Is there anything further to come before this meeting?" She paused. "If not, this concludes our business. Officers, present yourselves at the Altar for the closing ceremonies." She rapped the gavel twice.

I waited, eager to return to the room.

Beth finally said, "We are about to leave this Auxiliary room. Let us endeavor to regulate our conduct so it will bring honor to our organization. I now declare this meeting closed with the retiring of the Colors." She announced when the next meeting would be held.

Moments later, the meeting room door opened.

"Does this happen at every meeting?" I whispered to Jo after walking back into the room to join her.

She nodded and whispered back, "Beth is by the book. I'm all for what the organization represents, but she can be over the top."

"Can you introduce me? I want to catch her before she leaves."

"Sure thing." Jo looked over to where Beth stood. "In just a minute. She's talking to Cal Stanton."

Beth was an attractive woman in her forties. Her husband Michael was at least ten years older than her, and not very attractive himself. He definitely had a thing for younger women. I was guessing his power made him attractive enough. I watched Beth smile and laugh with Cal, who looked to be around her age and very handsome.

"Isn't he the head of the American Legion?" I asked.

"He sure is," Jo replied. "They've worked on many projects together over the years." She lowered her voice. "I've seen them in Smokey Jo's before," she made a set of air quotes as she added, "working." She raised her auburn eyebrow high.

"Interesting." I grabbed Jo's arm and pulled her with me. "I say we work our way on over there."

We had almost reached Beth and Cal when Michael McMasters walked in with a young man beside him.

I stopped in my tracks.

"What's wrong?" Jo asked.

"That boy." I pointed.

"What about him?"

"He's the boy I saw in the woods with the twins. Danny is his name."

"I know."

"How do you know him?"

"Because, Sunny." Jo looked me in the eye. "That's Danny McMasters. Councilman Michael and Beth McMasters son."

Michael spotted me and stiffened. Danny looked at me, and his eyes grew huge. Beth studied her husband and son, then turned her gaze on me and frowned. They seemed to communicate silently with each other, collectively turning about face in a unified front and leaving together, post haste.

Cal Stanton watched them leave. He glanced in our direction and shrugged, then headed down the street in the other direction.

Jo looked at me, and I looked at her, then as if reading each other's minds, we both said in unison, "And the plot thickens."

"THINGS ARE JUST GETTING WEIRD," I SAID TO MITCH AT Smokey Jo's Tavern. We were having dinner after my attempt at making homemade meatloaf with mashed potatoes had nearly burnt our house down.

I snagged a French fry off my husband's plate, and he pushed the carrots and celery sticks in my direction. I leveled him with my *seriously* look. He slid a cup of blue cheese at me and shrugged over my frown. That was his idea of a compromise.

"You're eating for two," he said. "I'm thinking my son might need more than grease to develop."

"And I'm thinking my daughter will be like her mama and thrive on eating whatever she pleases."

"Fine with me, as long as *he* gets vegetables, too, like his daddy."

"I'll meet you halfway and eat the vegetables, Daddy, if you throw in dessert."

He winked. "You got it, Mama."

I melted, my heart full with the realization that we were more than just husband and wife now. We were a family. A growing family that I was becoming more and more happy about every day.

"Wow." Jo set a piece of apple pie ala mode on the

bar in front of me. "Maybe you really are eating for two...as in twins."

"Don't say that, Jo." Mitch pushed his plate away as if he'd lost his appetite. "I'm barely used to the idea of one."

"Don't worry, buddy," Cole said, wiping down the counter before us, then slinging his towel over his shoulder as he reached for Mitch's plate. "It's not that bad. I've got your back if you need me."

I snagged the plate and slid it in my direction, looking more like I was a food critic with all the dishes before me than just a pregnant lady.

Cole held up his hands. "Hey, I know better than to take a pregnant woman's food away before she's finished." Jo grabbed her own unfinished plate, sending her husband a glare. "Or a nursing mom's." He scrubbed a palm over his buzz cut and winced at Mitch. "Sorry to tell you, buddy, but you won't understand the language even after they give birth."

"Great," was all my husband said.

"Moving on," Jo replied.

"What are we moving on from?" Sean asked, coming out of the kitchen, carrying clean glasses to restock.

"Women," Mitch stated.

"Babies," Cole added.

"Nightmares," Sean confirmed.

"Doghouses." Zoe crossed her arms, standing right behind Sean.

"Going now, lass." Sean walked past her in a wide arc, saying over his shoulder, "Pray for me, boys."

"Forget that, I'm coming with you." Cole grabbed a tub and carried dirty dishes with him as he lengthened his strides.

"Wise decision, Sasquatch." Jo wiped her mouth as she finished her dinner.

The girls and I looked at Mitch.

"What's that, boys?" he hollered, looking toward the door to the silent kitchen. He stood and made his way to the back saying to us, "Sorry, ladies, they need my help."

"Sure they do." Jo grunted and shook her head.

"What a weird day today has been." I dug into my dessert, amazed at how much I was able to eat yet not get full.

"In all seriousness, do you think you have any new evidence that will point the direction away from my fiancé?" Zoe asked, chewing her bottom lip.

"We have a few leads we're looking into," I responded.

"I think I just found you one more," Jo added.

"What do you mean?" Zoe asked.

Jo jerked her head to the side, and we looked in that direction. Willow Goodbody sat at a booth in the far corner of the room, her head tipped closely to Greg Gates. Greg didn't have an alibi for the night of the murder, claiming he was looking for Sean all night and then went home alone. Meanwhile, Willow had said she spent the night with Dawson. She did, but she didn't get there until one a.m. The murder happened between eleven p.m. and twelve a.m., thereby canceling her alibi. Greg didn't seem too broken up over Audra, and Willow had certainly moved on from Dawson pretty quickly.

The question was, what were they doing together.

12

"The baby's heartbeat is strong, so that's good, but your blood pressure is elevated a little," Tina Doolittle-Wilcox said to me as she pulled off the blood pressure cuff. She'd put her own personal spin on her exam rooms, painting them a pale lilac with green polka dots. I loved it, but I didn't love the news she'd just given me.

Tina was a curvy, short, brunette with an infectious personality, who'd had a thing for Doctor Wilcox for years. He was a green-eyed, blond-haired Ken doll come to life. She had been his nurse since he'd opened his practice and had been there for him throughout everything he'd gone through. He'd been in love with the local librarian back then, but she'd never returned the affection. After she was murdered, he finally noticed what he had right in front of him, and the rest was history.

Tina had since then gotten certified as a nurse practitioner and a midwife. They'd been married for six months, and she was a full-fledged practitioner now, no longer just his nurse. After my mother had tried to fix me up with Doc when I'd first come to Divinity, it seemed weird for him to deliver my baby. So, I'd opted to go with Tina.

"Sunny, did you hear me?" Tina studied me with concern. "Are you okay?"

"Sorry." I rubbed my head. "Pregnancy brain. It's been distracting me a lot lately."

"Ahhh," she responded knowingly. "Don't worry, it's not permanent."

"So, I've been told." I thought about her words, and I frowned. "What does me having high blood pressure mean? Aren't I too young for that?"

"No, actually. Many things can elevate a person's blood pressure. Stress and diet are big factors." She tapped her clipboard. "It simply means, you need to relax and watch your diet, especially salt."

I sucked in a breath. "No more fries?" Crossing my fingers, I prayed I heard her wrong wrong.

"No more fries," she responded in a no-nonsense way.

I dropped my arms and sighed. "Fine." I hung my head on a groan. "Mitch is going to love this, and I'm going to turn into a rabbit by the time he's done with me."

She laughed. "You don't have to just eat carrots and celery, and I'm not saying you can't ever have potatoes. Just try not to make them fried with salt on them all the time. Or at the very least, reserve that for an occasional treat."

A shred of hope filled my heart with happiness. "Deal," I agreed, thinking it was the little things that made life grand. "I am trying to learn how to cook," I offered as consolation, "but I think I need help. I'll have to have Great-Grandma Tootsie teach me. Granny Gert and Fiona are more about baking, and my mother doesn't have a clue in the kitchen."

"Sounds like a wise decision. I might join you. Those women sure do know the way to a man's heart." She leaned forward and lowered her voice. "Between you and me, I intend to keep my man very happy."

I laughed. "Trust me, my detective would be in heaven if I could learn how to cook the way the Trio does, and he didn't have to keep hunting for something edible."

"Amen, sister. My lovely doctor would be thrilled as well not to have to fix the dinners I make. They're edible, but nothing special."

"Speaking of people who fix things, do you know Rita Haynes?"

"Actually, yes. She's the mental health therapist my husband and I refer our patients to. They used to like her a lot, but I haven't heard much from them lately. From my own interactions with her, she seems like she knows her stuff. She doesn't have the warmest bedside manner, but she's direct and helpful." Tina eyed me curiously. "Why do you ask?"

"I went to see her to talk through some things that were bothering me. She actually helped, but you're right about the bedside manner. And let's just say, she's not a fan of psychics."

"I heard she was pretty upset when a few of her patients, who happened to also be patients in our practice, went to Audra for a reading."

"Yes, the Lowenthal twins. I talked to them. They were pretty upset with Audra's reading from a year ago and confronted her at the Psychic Fair. I've never seen girls that look so perfect. Their hair is amazing and their faces are flawless. They almost don't look real, like little porcelain dolls. Anyway, Rita was upset because the girls aren't the most mentally stable, and she was afraid Audra had preyed on their weaknesses."

"I can't comment on the girls' health because they're patients of ours, but I can tell you they're not the only clients of Rita's who jumped ship and went to Audra for help instead." I opened my mouth to ask who, but she held up her hand. "That's all I'm going to say about that. You'll have to talk to Rita if you want to know more."

"Oh, I plan to."

"Just don't overdo it." She typed something into my chart on the computer, and then said, "I want to see you back in a couple days to recheck that blood pressure. Keep meditating like we talked about, and make healthy choices." She winked.

"Thanks, Tina. I will." And I would also follow up with Rita for sure.

Why were people so willing to jump ship from her practice? I'd witnessed her hostility firsthand, and the woman was in great shape. Strong as many men, I bet. Maybe there was more going on with Rita than a poor bedside manner. Maybe she had more of a beef with Audra than we knew about.

Maybe it was time I found out.

———

"ARE YOU READY?" I ASKED MY MOTHER AS I PICKED HER up from the inn.

"Yes, thank you, darling," she responded, dusting off the seat and laying a paper towel down before climbing in, of course. "No way would I let your grandmother drive me in her hearse-mobile. That woman is a menace on the roads. Fiona isn't any better, and your father is too busy for me these days." My mother sniffed sharply.

"Really? How so?"

"He is being ridiculous, following Harry around on his quest to complete his bucket list. Now, mind you, Harry is a fit man for his age, but he's much older. I can see the rush for him. Your father has plenty of years left, so I don't know why he's acting crazy. At least, I hope he does." She pursed her lips, forming rare creases in her face. "You don't think there's something he's not telling me, do you?" My parents might not be the most loving parents, but they adored each other. I had always wanted a marriage like theirs.

"Dad, is fine, Mother."

She harumphed and looked out her window.

My father had always been Dad to me, but my mother preferred Mother. That pretty much summed up my relationship with my parents. My father was my big teddy bear, while my mother was, well, my mother.

"I think he's just having a lot of fun," I added. "He had a stressful job for so many years being a cardiologist."

She sat up straighter. "Well, I had a stressful job, too. Being a lawyer isn't easy, you know. I was up against sharks."

"Exactly," I said and meant it. "Did you ever think maybe you should join him? You might find yourself having some fun as well."

"Good Lord, no." She looked aghast. "You will never see me running around acting like a fool."

I thought of Mimi's Sound of Music spectacle, but wisely remained silent.

"Retirement has made him lose his mind," she went on. "Good thing our grandchild will have at least one grandparent who is sound of mind."

A warmth filled my chest. "You're really excited

about being a grandmother, aren't you?" I peeked at her sideways, curious to see her reaction.

"I will make a great Mimi," she said, looking straight ahead. "Like you said, I'm not in that stressful, time-consuming job anymore." She hesitated a moment, then added, "I wasn't around as much as I would have liked while you were growing up. It was difficult to be taken seriously as a woman in a man's world. I had to do things I didn't always like in order to get ahead." Her gaze met mine. "My only regret is not being there for you enough. I'm sorry, truly." She nodded once. "I won't make that mistake again."

I blinked tears away, unable to believe I was finally hearing the words I'd longed for my whole life.

"Sylvia," my mother shrieked, "watch the road."

I jerked my bug back into my lane, my heart pounding.

"Sorry, I meant Sunny." She cleared her throat.

"It's okay," I replied, and we both knew I was talking about more than my name. "Thank you, Mom. That means a lot." I glanced at her briefly and saw the tears in her own eyes. Staying focused on the road, we didn't speak the rest of the way in a comfortable silence.

I pulled into A Cut Above, the specialty deli that carried fancy foods Gretta's Grocery did not have in stock. Great-Grandma Tootsie's meals were based around down-home cooking while Granny Gert and Fiona's desserts rivaled Betty Crocker. My mother still added a touch of her own flair by offering special hors-d'oeuvres paired with aged wines and top-shelf spirits at select times every day.

We walked inside, and she headed straight for the cheese counter. I looked around the store and couldn't believe my eyes. Rich Hastings was over at the meat counter having what looked to be a charcuterie board prepared. Cured meats, cheeses, crackers, breads, fruit, nuts, olives and spreads were piled high on a wooden board. I made my way over, figuring this was my best opportunity to talk to him. It wasn't like he could leave until his order was done. At least, I was banking on that.

"Hi, Rich. I'm Sunny, Mark's friend." I figured saying Jo's name right now wasn't the smartest plan of attack.

He whipped around and stared wide-eyed at me for a moment, then narrowed his eyes. His whole body stiffened as he replied, "I know exactly who you are, Mrs. Stone, so you can skip the pretense. What do you want?"

"I saw you at the races talking to Mark."

He hesitated, then replied, "So, that's not a crime."

"Avoiding the police is. Last time I checked, you haven't been cleared to leave town other than going to your winery."

He rolled his bald head on his neck and stroked a hand over his goatee for a moment, as if thinking. "I'm not avoiding the police, and I have nothing to hide."

"Really, because no one knows where you were the night of Audra's murder. You were seen arguing with her pretty heatedly the first night of the Psychic Fair. What was that all about?"

His eyes hardened. "I don't have to tell you anything."

A trickle of unease traced across my scalp. I squashed my shiver and raised my chin a notch. "Then you'll have to tell my husband. You know, my *detective* husband. He's really big and kind of grumpy, especially when he's hungry. You don't even want to know." I swiped my hand through the air. "I mean, I thought I could eat a lot, but that man can eat—"

Rich looked at me like I was having a spell. "Is this going to take long?"

"Anyway, where was I?" I strummed my fingertips, trying to regain my train of thought. "Oh, yeah. Do you really want to go through this interrogation again? If you tell me where you were, I'll relay the information to him." I tapped my chest, and pulled out my handy dandy notebook. "I'm officially a consultant for the Divinity Police Department, so they'll believe what I tell them."

Rich closed his gaping jaw and shrugged, probably figuring it was easier to just answer me than listen to me ramble on anymore. "It's no secret I didn't like Audra Grimshaw. Look, I'm just trying to make a living like everyone else. This winery means everything to me. I've poured my heart and soul into it. The Psychic Fair was one of my first opportunities to introduce my wines and pick up new venders. Audra told everyone at the Psychic Fair that my wine is no good. Then to make matters worse, Sean ratted me out to Mrs. West that I mixed up her orders."

"Twice," I added.

"Whatever, I'm new to this." He shoved his hands in his jean's pockets. "I was working things out, but no one is giving me a chance."

"She has a business to run. You can't blame her." I kind of felt bad for the guy. "Maybe you should get some help on the creative side. It might help improve your wines."

His gaze narrowed. "Why, you didn't like the wine either?"

I could truthfully answer, thank goodness. "I'm pregnant. I never tried your wine. I'm just saying if others are expressing that they don't like something, maybe hire some help who know what they're doing."

"Easier said than done. All of that takes money, Mrs. Stone." He tapped *his* chest. "Money I don't have. I've sunk everything I own into this business and haven't seen a profit yet."

"Is that why you were at the racetrack?"

His eyes shifted about. "There's nothing illegal about placing a bet."

"No there's not, but the odds of winning are slim."

And there was that hard look again. "You let me worry about that."

"I was just trying to help." I flipped my notebook open. "You still haven't said where you were the night of Audra's murder."

"I might not have liked Audra, but I'm not a murderer. I ran into Mark, and we went back to his place to have a few drinks and talk about the upcoming racing season. He offered to let me sleep over because we'd had a few too many. I accepted. End of story."

"I'll have to check out your alibi, you know. Before the story can end, I mean." If he was lying, this was his last chance to change his mind and come clean.

"Check away, Mrs. Stone. Mark will verify everything I said." Rich paid for his order. "If we're done here, am I free to go?"

"You've always been free to go." I flipped my notebook closed and put it away. "And if your alibi checks out, you'll be free to leave town."

"Oh, it will check out. And if I never see any of you again, that will be fine by me." He turned around and walked with long, purposeful strides out the door, pulling out his phone along the way.

"Are you okay, Sunny?" my mother asked, hurrying

over to me. "That man gives me the creeps. Olivia says he's bad news."

"There's definitely something off about him." I watched him disappear down the street, lost in conversation as he walked. "I'm fine, but thanks for asking, Mom." Her face flushed over my use of Mom again, and I felt the ice surrounding my heart regarding my mother begin to thaw. For the first time in too many years to remember, I felt hope for the future of our relationship.

"Well, I'm ready when you are. I've got everything I needed."

"Me too," I said, "I think it's time for a visit to the vet."

"Oh, no," my mother said with genuine concern in her voice. "Is there something wrong with Morty?"

There was a time I never thought I would hear words like that coming from my mother's mouth. It warmed my heart even further knowing they had a special bond now.

"Morty's fine," I replied reassuringly, watching her shoulders wilt with relief. "I'm talking about an equestrian vet."

My mother wrinkled her forehead. "Are you thinking about buying a horse?"

"Let's just say I have some questions only Dr. Mark Silverman can answer."

13

I dropped my mother off at the inn, and she insisted I go inside for lunch. When I relayed what Tina Wilcox had said, my mother was pleased as punch to have Toots make me a low sodium soup and salad. She didn't say I told you so, which was a step in the right direction, even though I could tell she was mentally saying it. She ordered me to go home and take a nap, which I said I would, then I promptly headed in the other direction.

Equine vets normally called on their patients rather than the other way around, mostly due to the sheer size of their clientele. I was taking a chance that Mark wouldn't even be at his office. I parked in front then made my way inside. To my surprise, he was in his office with the door slightly ajar.

And he wasn't alone.

I stepped quietly closer to the door and listened.

"I don't understand why he can't win anymore. He was doing so well," said a familiar male voice.

"He's a little fatigued," Mark replied. "Maybe you should keep him out of the next race and let his body recover."

"I can't afford to do that, and you know it."

"All I know is you won't have a horse left to race if you don't take this seriously. You can't push him to the degree you're pushing him. It's not safe."

"Well, I don't have any other horses ready to race. He's my only hope, so please try to think of anything that might help him."

"Short of rest, I'm not sure what else I can do. I'm not a miracle worker, but I'll try. You gave me my start, Mr. Ventura. I won't forget that."

"Thank you, Mark. I don't mean to snap. I'm just getting desperate."

"Understood, sir."

Mark opened the door, and I took a quick step back, inspecting a magazine and pretending to study the décor.

"Mrs. Stone, I can't imagine what you're doing here, but it's always a pleasure," Mark said, sounding sincere.

"Please, call me Sunny." I smiled at him and looked at Antonio, widening my smile. "Mr. Ventura, it's good to see you." I peeked around him. "Where's Sweet Life? I can't imagine he could hide very well." I laughed.

"The animals don't come to see me, Sunny. I make house calls."

"I know that, I'm just messing with you."

Neither man smiled.

"Alrighty, then." My smile faded.

"Dr. Silverman was just discussing a plan of action with me for Sweet Life," Antonio said, reaching out and giving my arm a squeeze. "It's good to see you, Mrs. Stone. Say hello to Mitch for me, would you? You've got a good one there."

"I will," I patted his hand, "and I really do wish you luck with the rest of the season." Mitch was right. Antonio was such a nice guy. I felt bad for him to be down on his luck and having horse troubles on top of that.

"Thank you." He nodded once, then left the office, his shoulders slumped.

"Seriously, Sunny, how can I help you?" Mark said after Antonio left.

"I know you're not a small animal vet, but Morty's been acting really strange. What do you think could be wrong?"

Mark thought about it and then said, "He might be jealous. You're pregnant, and animals can sense that. New husband, new baby...his world's about to change."

"Thanks, Doc. That helps."

"Maybe give him some extra attention."

"I'm trying, if he ever stays home long enough."

"I have to ask. Why come to me?" Mark looked at me curiously. "Don't you go to Dr. Sherry Parker for Morty issues?"

"Yes, but I needed to talk to you about something else. When I got here, I couldn't help overhearing your conversation with Antonio." A suspicious look crossed Mark's face. "Is Sweet Life really in danger of getting seriously injured or worse if he keeps racing?" I quickly asked while I still could.

His demeaner changed to a not-so-great bedside manner. "I can't discuss my clients with you, Sunny."

"I mean, if Mr. Ventura is having money problems, there has to be another way to get by. Surely nothing is worth risking his horse's life."

"He's got it covered." Mark turned away and started packing up. "There's nothing for you to worry about, Sunny. Now, how can I possibly help you?"

"No, I'm not in the market for a horse. One mysterious cat is enough for me." I snorted a laugh. Again, no smile. Geesh. "Anyway, I'm here because I talked to Rich Hastings."

A flash of something crossed over Mark's face, but it was so brief, I couldn't tell what it was. "And what does Mr. Hastings have to do with me?"

"Well, he says on the night of Audra's murder, he was with you. That the two of you went back to your place to have drinks and discuss the racing season."

Mark's face didn't move an inch. No reaction at all as he said, "That is correct. We talked for a while that night."

"You're sure about that?"

He nodded.

"Because obstructing justice is against the law, you know," I felt the need to point out since he was friends with Zoe and Jo.

"I'm not obstructing justice, Mrs. Stone." He gave me a disapproving look. "I did in fact discuss the races with Mr. Hastings. Now if you'll excuse me, I have a farm I need to visit." He picked up his vet bag and headed out of his office door.

"By all means." I followed him outside.

He locked up and left, acting as if everything was all right, but my gut had never steered me wrong. Everything was not all right with his story. Something was very wrong.

I watched him disappear down the street, and then I turned around to head to my VW Bug. Who I saw leaning against the driver's side door made me jump. Oh, boy, I was right. This was not good. I took a deep breath and slowly put one foot in front of the other as I made my way across the parking lot.

I was in big trouble, and didn't dare make eye contact. I had no idea what to say, but that didn't stop the man who stood before me.

"Start talking, Tink. You've got some explaining to do."

———

TURNED OUT MY HUSBAND HAD STOPPED BY MY mother's, who happily filled him in on what Tina Wilcox had said. Then she told him I had gone home to take a nap. How was I supposed to know when I told her that little fib that he would be working from home? After she confided in him about my comment regarding going to see an equine vet, he knew exactly what I was up to, and he didn't like it one bit.

After Dawson, I had promised my husband I wouldn't investigate on my own. He had resigned himself to the fact that Captain Walker wanted me as a consultant on this case, but the days of him being okay with me questioning people alone were over. Being pregnant had changed things in his eyes. I wasn't just putting myself in danger, I was putting our child in danger. Ours, as in part his, and according to his irrational logic, he had fifty percent say in what I did.

I humored him and let him think that.

No way was I waiting around for him to tell me what to do. Sometimes opportunities presented themselves that couldn't wait for him to be available. I had filled him in on everything at the vet's office, and then drove my own car home so he could cool off and come to grips with me being a big girl who could take care of herself.

I got out of my VW Bug, and he climbed out of his truck. This was the moment of truth. We faced off. He put his hands on his hips, and I crossed my arms over my chest. We both just stared at each other. Finally, he sighed and started walking over to me. I started walking, too, willing to meet him in the middle.

He looked deep into my eyes with his stormy gray intense ones, then shook his head as his whole face softened. He kissed me on the lips, then said, "Quit giving me gray hairs, woman," and then he disappeared into his mancave of a garage.

I didn't say a word because I honestly couldn't promise he wouldn't be completely gray by the time this case was solved. I blew a kiss toward the garage and then headed for the front door. I stopped short.

Zoe sat on our porch.

"Hey, you. I didn't even notice your car. How long have you been here?" I asked as I unlocked the door and let us both inside.

"Not long." She took a quivering breath. "I needed girl talk. I know how busy Jo is with the twins and work, so I thought of you."

"I'm glad you did." I headed for the kitchen. "I'll make us some tea."

She sat down at the table while I brewed us both some chamomile. When it was ready, I joined her.

"I'm just so worried that everything we had planned for our future will never happen." She dipped her tea bag in the hot water.

"You don't believe he had an affair with Audra, do you?" I blew on my tea and took a sip, holding the warm mug between my palms.

"No, I know he could never murder anyone," she replied with conviction. "Honestly, I know in my heart he will always be faithful to me. Sean may have been a ladies' man, but he has never been a liar or a cheat."

"Oh, honey, Mitch and I are working hard to find

the real killer." I reached out and held her hand. "I hope you know that."

"I do," she squeezed once then let go, "but I know that no matter how much you guys believe in Sean's innocence, it's not enough. Didn't Mitch say the coroner ruled that Audra was strangled before being pushed into the puddle, making it look like electrocution?" I nodded, and she continued, "I've watched enough crime shows to know that indicates a crime of passion. Sean was furious with her. Everyone heard them argue, and then witnesses heard him come back after the fight and threaten her to stay away from us or else." Zoe fought back tears. "He's certainly strong enough to strangle someone."

"That's true, but so are many other people."

"We might all believe him, but the facts are making him look so guilty. What do I do if he gets convicted of a murder he didn't commit?"

"I know I keep making these promises, but I'm telling you I have a feeling everything's going to be okay. My gut never lies."

"Okay, that makes me feel better. Not better enough to plan my wedding." She shuddered. "I can't even think about that." She took another sip of her tea and looked reflective. "I don't feel so hopeless now. Thank you for that. I needed this."

"Good. I'm glad." I finished my tea and put my cup in the sink. "I helped Sean to relax. Did he tell you?"

"Yes! And just so you know, he meditates every day now. I feel so helpless. I wish I could ease his worries somehow."

"Just be there for him. That's all he needs."

She nodded, finishing her tea and putting her cup in the sink as well. "Can you teach me how to meditate?"

"Sure thing." I walked her into my sanctuary where my yoga mats were and went over all the things I had told Sean.

I instructed her to sit in a full lotus position with her feet on top of her knees, because frankly, Zoe was much more flexible than Sean and did yoga regularly.

"How do you want my hands?"

"The thumb represents fire which is a symbol of power and transformation. Fire represents strength, which you need right now. You also need to lighten the weight on your shoulders and decrease your anxiety. Your index finger represents air which is your life force. Air is purifying and will increase your lightness in life. So, let's join your thumb and index finger together and rest your hands on your knees."

"I'm ready," she said.

"Okay." I sat facing her with our knees touching, trying to transfer some of my own strength to her. "Breathe in and out slowly. Focus on your breathing, and empty your mind. Clear your thoughts. Allow your body to be centered and grounded."

We breathed for a while, each of us lost in our own worlds, when, suddenly, I was jerked into tunnel vision. Flashes of babies kept swirling around me, and there were always two of them. The words two babies kept repeating in the distance like a chant. My head was spinning with confusion.

"Sunny, can you hear me? Sunny, you're scaring me. Are you okay?"

I shook my head and came out of the vision. Zoe had moved away so our knees lost contact.

"Sorry, I just had a vision."

"Oh, wow, I had no idea your visions looked like that."

I took a moment to just breathe and calm my

racing heart. "They take a lot out of me physically as well. I go through everything the person I'm seeing did."

"What did you see?"

"Two babies. I keep seeing two babies." My eyes met hers. "Only, this time our knees were touching."

Her eyebrows disappeared into her hairline. "What does that mean?"

"I think the two babies has to do with you," I said carefully. "Maybe you're going to have twins someday."

She waved off that notion and grabbed my hands. "All I've wished for is a sign that will help us prove someone else killed Audra."

"You think the Lowenthal twins killed her?" I pondered her words, having once considered that myself. "But she was strangled."

"Like you said, many people are strong enough to do that. Besides, they have a buddy who would literally do anything for them," Zoe pointed out.

"Danny." She had a point.

"Exactly." She smiled.

"He says he's their alibi, but like you said, he would do anything for them." My mind was swirling with possibilities to check out. "Speaking of alibis. I went to see Mark today. That's where I was coming from when I pulled in."

"Why did you go to see him? You're not buying a horse, are you?"

"Good Lord, no. Why does everyone think that? I can barely handle my cat. Can you imagine the trouble I would get into with a horse?"

She laughed.

Now here was someone who got my humor. "I ran into Rich Hastings at A Cut Above this morning when

I was there shopping with my mother. I had a great talk with her, by the way."

"Oh, that's great." Zoe clapped her hands. "I can't wait to hear all about that, but first, finish your story, please," she added gently.

"I swear this pregnancy brain is going to do me in." I rubbed my temples. "Anyway, Rich gave me an alibi for the night of Audra's murder."

"What was it?"

"He said he was with Mark at his apartment, having drinks and talking about the racing season. Said he had too much to drink and spent the night."

"Wait." Zoe wrinkled up her face in confusion. "No, he didn't."

"Why do you say that?"

"Because Mark Facetimed me right after everyone left when the storm hit. He suspected I would be upset after Greg Gates' accusation that Sean had an affair with Audra, and then they got in that big fight. Mark wasn't wrong." Zoe shrugged. "I was upset, and Mark and I have history. He's a friend. So, I took the Face-time call. I told Sean not to come home because I was angry, but I didn't expect him to actually listen to me. When I couldn't reach him, I became really upset. Mark stayed on the phone with me for hours, mostly with him consoling me." Her gaze met mine. "Sunny, trust me, he was alone the whole time. That can only mean one thing."

"Rich Hastings is a liar." And Mark Silverman bla-tantly covered up for him.

14

The next day, Mitch and I pulled into the Town Hall parking lot. He cut the engine to his truck, and we waited. Mitch had gone over Audra's phone records, and one phone number kept coming up over and over. It turned out the phone wasn't traceable.

It was a burner phone.

"Do you really think the phone belongs to Michael McMasters?" I asked.

"You said you saw him with Audra in your vision, right?"

"Yes?" I answered, waiting for the catch. I knew my husband loved me, but he wasn't a full believer in my abilities.

"Then that's good enough for me."

"Seriously?" A lump formed in my throat over words I'd never expected to hear. My husband was finally a true believer.

"I don't exactly know how you know the things you do, but I can't deny there's some truth in what you see."

"And *that* my darling detective is good enough for me."

He winked, and my heart melted.

"So, if Michael McMasters was having an affair with Audra, it would make sense for him to use a burner phone. He wouldn't want to risk his reputation getting damaged if word got out. Being married to a prominent lady like Beth and having a son would make the affair even more scandalous."

"The fact that Audra was pregnant when she died and that she claimed the baby was Michael's isn't something he can hide for long if Greg shares Audra's diary," I said.

"The coroner's report revealed she was pregnant."

My jaw fell open. "Why didn't you tell me?"

"Call it a test." Mitch shrugged. "I wanted to see what you could find on your own. And you found plenty. The police didn't know the baby could be Michael McMasters. Your vision implicated him in the affair. It's part of what made me finally believe in your psychic ability and the value you have to consulting with my department."

"Well, thank you, then."

"You're welcome." He winked. "That diary is the proof we need that Michael McMasters was the father of Audra's baby."

"In the meantime, the question is, did Audra tell him about the baby the night she died, and that's what pushed him to lose control and kill her?"

The Town Hall meeting ended, and people started filing out of the building. Michael headed to his car and left in a hurry.

"Only one way to find out." Mitch started the engine and followed him.

Michael didn't turn down the street to his house. Instead, he kept going down Main Street in the shopping section of Divinity. He pulled into Eddy's Gun

Emporium, and Mitch followed. He parked, and we waited until Michael went inside.

After a few minutes, we followed him in.

Michael stood at the counter, looking agitated as he inspected a couple different handguns with Eddy.

"I didn't know you had a pistol permit, Mr. Mc-Masters," Mitch said as he came to a stop behind him.

Michael whipped around and stared at him, then his gaze landed on me and his eyes widened. "Yes, Detective, I do. My family consists of a long line of hunters. I've never felt the need to carry one until now."

"You do know you need a concealed carry in order to carry one on your person," Mitch responded.

"I've already applied. I figured I could at least purchase my gun with my pistol permit and keep it at the house to defend myself should the need arise."

"Why would the need arise? This is Divinity we're talking about." Mitch eyed him closely.

"Exactly." His gaze landed on me and hardened. "Not a safe place since *she* came to town."

"Easy, pal." Mitch's tone was laced with steel as he stepped in front of me. "That's my wife you're talking about."

"Hey." I peeked around my husband's side. "The recent string of murders isn't my fault." Ducking under his arm, I stepped forward by his side once more.

Mitch frowned.

Michael stabbed his finger in my direction. "*She* was the only other person besides Greg Gates who knew about Audra's diary. Now the whole town knows."

Mitch clenched his fists and opened his mouth.

I stepped in front of him this time. "Look, Mr. Mc-

Masters. I didn't say a word except to my husband. If word got out, then it had to be Mr. Gates who talked."

"Yeah, well now, the whole town is angry with me. My wife is a beloved member of the community." Michael started to pace. "This is going to be horrible for my career."

"Maybe you should have thought of that before sleeping around on your wife," Mitch pointed out, "twice."

Michael stopped pacing and looked at my husband. "Trust me when I say, my wife is no innocent. She was fully aware of my indiscretions. She has plenty of her own. Our marriage is an open one, so long as we don't bring scandal to our family name. That was the deal. Yet the town doesn't see it that way, and she's not helping by not coming to my defense. They all think I'm the only guilty party here."

"Then why not blow her in?" Mitch asked.

"I won't do that to my son, Danny." Michael exhaled. "I haven't been around much in his life. Work always got in the way. He's angry with me, but he worships his mother. I won't take that away from him."

I thought of my own mother. She would never have an affair, but even she admitted work made it difficult to be around much in my life. I could understand the anger and frustration Danny had for his father. I had to admit it was admirable for Michael to want to protect his son. At least he was finally putting someone else first before himself.

"You used Audra years ago when she was dating Sean," I said. "Did she get pregnant on purpose this time in hopes of getting you to leave your wife?"

"I don't know what went through the mind of that woman. She was beautiful, I'll give you that, but she was evil." He shuddered. "I would never have broken up my family for the likes of her, yet she refused to leave me alone."

"I think she told you she was pregnant, and you bought a burner phone to harass her. When that didn't work, you panicked." Mitch took a step toward Michael. "You lost control and strangled her to stop her from ruining your life, then tried to make it look like an accident by pushing her into the electrified puddle by her car."

"You're crazy. I don't know what phone you're talking about. The only phone I have is my personal phone." Michael took a step back, his eyes wary. "I didn't know anything about the pregnancy until Greg Gates told me in the grocery store. *He's* the angry one. If anyone is capable of murder, it would be him. He certainly had motive."

"Where were you between the hours of eleven p.m. and twelve a.m. that evening?" I asked.

"At home. The Psychic Fair had turned into a disaster after the storm hit, so I went straight home to bed. You can ask my housekeeper. She'll verify my alibi."

"Why not ask your wife?"

"Maybe it's time you asked my wife exactly what she's been up to lately." Michael picked up his purchase and headed for the door, adding over his shoulder, "Because she never came home that night."

THAT EVENING, JO, COLE, MITCH AND I WENT TO THE American Legion for drinks. You only needed one member, and both Jo and Cole belonged because of their family connections to the military, so Mitch and I could join them.

"This is actually really nice in here, and everything is so inexpensive," I said as I sat on my barstool with a mocktail in hand.

"Hey, don't get any ideas about leaving Smokey Jo's," Jo said with mock sternness, then sipped her gin and tonic.

"Nothing compares to your place, Jo." Mitch raised his beer in cheers, then took a long drink.

"It's not bad," Cole wisely agreed, setting his beer in front of him.

It didn't have the ambiance that Smokey Jo's had, but it did have a sort of rustic charm with a big American flag over the top of the bar. And many of the regulars were old timers from around town. Harry and my father walked in, surprising us.

"Well, there's our boy," my father boomed, joining us at the bar and putting his arm around Mitch. "My favorite son-in-law."

"He's your only son-in-law, Dad." I rolled my eyes.

"He's still my favorite." My father let out a hearty laugh.

Mitch chuckled. "And you would be my favorite father-in-law."

"What would I be?" Harry asked, not to be outdone.

"My favorite uncle?" Mitch shrugged.

"Uncle Harry. I like that, boy." Harry slapped Mitch on the back. "Is the honeymoon over enough yet that you can join us fishing?"

"Bite your tongue, you old rascal," Jo chimed in. "Don't you know the honeymoon is never over."

"Oh, I know." Harry cackled then sobered. "Don't tell Fiona I said that."

"My lips are sealed." Jo winked at him.

"What are you guys up to?" Cole asked.

"We're on a pub crawl." My father beamed, puffing out his chest.

"That's right," Harry agreed. "It's on the bucket list." He pulled out a piece of paper. "Number twenty."

Good lord, they actually had a list. Harry's words registered. "You've done twenty bucket list items since my father retired?"

Harry nodded, standing a little straighter and grinning wide.

"Isn't it grand?" My father's grin matched Harry's.

"No wonder Mom is having fits."

"Bah, she'll get over it." My father leaned closer to me. "I'm proud of you for talking to your mother. She seems lighter. Happier."

"I'm happier too," I said and realized I meant it.

The men all started talking about fishing and hunting and sports. Jo and I excused ourselves to go to the ladies' room. When we came out of the restroom, Cal Stanton walked in as expected and sat at a table by himself. He placed an order with a waitress, then kept checking his watch.

I nudged Jo's arm. "Look who it is."

"Let's go talk to him." She glanced at the bar and shook her head. "They won't realize we're gone for a while."

We walked over to Cal's table, and he looked up in surprise.

"Well, hello, Ms. Burnham—er—West. I haven't seen you in a while. How's your father?"

"Hello yourself, Mr. Stanton," Jo replied. "My father and brothers are good. Same as always. Being loud and raising a ruckus."

He laughed. "That sounds just like them. Tell them I said hello."

"Will do." She pulled out a chair. "Mind if we sit down?"

He checked his watch once more then shrugged. "Sure. I'm supposed to be meeting Mrs. McMasters to discuss a combined fundraiser we're co-chairing, but she must be running late." He looked at me. "Who's your friend?"

"This is Sunny Stone."

"I heard Detective Stone got married." He held out his hand. "It's nice to meet you, Mrs. Stone."

I shook his hand. "It's very nice to meet you as well. Would you mind if we asked you some questions?" I pulled out my notebook.

"I don't see why not. What's this about?"

"I'm sure you've heard the rumors by now that Michael McMasters was having an affair with Audra and she was pregnant with his child when she was murdered."

He nodded. "Terrible scandal. Beth is a mess over it. It's a big embarrassment for her, given her standing in this community."

"Michael claims he's not the only one who cheated. That Beth was having an affair as well." I scanned my notes, then looked him in the eye. "With you."

"I don't have anything to hide, Mrs. Stone. It's no secret I've loved Beth for the better half of my life. She was never unfaithful to Michael until he cheated on her first and then claimed he wanted an open marriage. I know she loves me, too. I thought maybe she would leave him for me, but after Danny came along, she refused."

"Michael says Beth never came home the night of Audra's murder. She certainly could have been angry enough over Audra's pregnancy to want to kill her.

Maybe she found out about the pregnancy and bought a burner phone to harass her. Then when that didn't work, she might have confronted her the night of the storm and lost control and killed her to put a stop from the scandal coming out once and for all."

"Beth is not a killer, and I've seen her phone. I've never seen her carry another phone of any kind. Besides, she was with me all night long that night."

"I think you would say anything to keep your lover out of trouble."

"And I think this conversation is over." He gave Jo a hard, disappointed look and then left the legion in a huff.

"Sorry, Jo," I said.

"Don't be. You didn't ask anything the police wouldn't ask, and it's Cal fault for getting mixed up in the mess to start with."

"Something tells me there's more to their story."

"I think you need to hear Beth McMaster's side. And lucky for you, I know exactly where to find her." Jo looked at me with a mischievous grin. "But you're not gonna like it one bit."

15

"You have got to be kidding me." I looked up at the Wally's World sign and whined. Who worked out this early? The sun was barely up. Let's just say I was not an early riser. I was having a pity party of one because Jo and Zoe were having none of it.

"You'll thank me later," Jo said. "Giving birth is no joke. You're going to need your strength."

"I don't think I'll ever have kids." Zoe shuddered.

"Yes, you will," Jo said. "You'll see."

"Why today?" I groaned. "I have plenty of time to get strong."

"First, I need to get into shape because Cole surprised me with a getaway trip, adults only." Jo wagged her eyebrows. "Second, it's never too early to get your body baby ready." Jo grabbed my arm and pulled me with her, while Zoe took my other arm and ushered me through the front door. "Third, Beth McMasters takes this Zumba class every week. Granny Gert and Fiona told me."

"You mean they're here, too?" I gaped. "I thought they had class on a different day and time?"

"They've been regulars at this class since they were

the Dynamic Duo," Zoe said. "Now that they're the Tasty Trio, they asked Great-Grandma Tootsie, but it's a bit too much for her given she's turning one hundred this year."

"Please don't tell me my mother is here."

"That would be a hard no," Jo said. "Yoga is more your mother's speed."

"At least I have one less person to humiliate myself in front of."

Zoe grabbed towels for all of us, and we slipped into the back of the room seconds before Jerry Lee Lewis blared through the speakers.

"Come on, ladies, you've got this. Move those hips. Let's salsa," Wally barked like a drill sergeant. He was a six-foot-eight-inch hairless God with silky milk-chocolate skin. For such a big man, he was surprisingly light on his feet.

Beth stood in the front row with Granny Gert and Fiona flanking her. Beth was in perfect step with every move, of course. Granny and Fiona bebopped beside her, making up their own moves while hooting and hollering every few seconds. They once told me Wally didn't care what they did as long as they moved. Jo and Zoe caught on pretty easily. I on the other hand looked like Elaine from Seinfeld. They went left, I went right. They stepped forward, I stepped back. My thumbs, hips and feet were moving non-stop, twisting in every direction like a snake writhing in pain. I was sure it was painful to watch.

How did I let them talk me into this? I mentally wailed.

"And shake it, Ladies. Shake it to the left, shake it to the right, shake shake shake it all night."

Good Lord, I was going to shake something loose

at this point. *Sorry, baby.* I patted my tummy, completely out of breath now.

"Twist and shout!"

I twisted, then shouted out in pain. These people were nuts.

"And two step now." Wally led the group in a circle around the room. "Put some heart into it, ladies. Let me see what you're made of."

I didn't want to risk Beth slipping out before we could talk to her again, so I started two-stepping my way double-time, way ahead of the beat, to the front of the class. I looked like an out-of-control windup toy, hopping more than stepping as I moved.

Jo gaped at me, and Zoe cringed.

I jerked my head toward Beth, hoping they'd get the hint.

People must have thought that was the next move because everyone in the class started bobbing their heads to the side.

"Bow to your partner and do-se-do."

What was this, the square dance ranch? I felt like I was back in high school gym class, and no better at dancing now than I was then.

Granny Gert and Fiona flanked me. Granny hooked my arm and spun me in a circle, passing me off to Fiona who spun me in the other direction. I was so dizzy when they let go right in front of Beth, I flew forward with flailing arms, taking out a few women along the way and flattening Beth like a pancake on the floor with me on top instead of a cherry.

The connection was instant.

My eyes narrowed into tunnel vision like they always did when I was having a vision. I emerged in a hospital room. Once again, I saw two babies in basinets. I felt joy and so much love. Then shame and guilt. Finally, a sadness so strong it made my heart ache and eyes fill with tears. Then anger and resentment. So much bitterness, my stomach turned sour. I wasn't whole anymore, and it was all his fault.

"Is she hurt?"

"She's crying."

"Oh, no. The other one's not breathing."

"Call an ambulance."

I blinked back to the present and looked at the wide-eyed blue-faced woman beneath me then around at the circle of familiar faces staring at us. The realization hit that I was still at the gym...on top of Beth McMasters...who was in dire need of oxygen. I rolled off the poor woman who immediately gasped for air.

Wally cut the music. "I think that's enough for today, ladies." He knelt by Beth and me. "Are you okay, Mrs. McMasters?"

"I think so," she said when she could finally breathe again.

He looked at me as I sat there, leaning back on my arms and panting like a dog that had just finished an agility course. "I'm surprised to see you here, Sunny. Are you okay? You're crying."

I nodded, unable to speak yet, and wiped my eyes from the vision I'd just had.

"Maybe you should start with a class that isn't so— er—challenging."

"Good idea," I finally replied. "Don't know what I was thinking?"

"I have a feeling I do," Beth muttered and let Wally help her to her feet.

Granny and Fiona helped me to mine.

"Oh, dear me, are you okay, Sunny?" Granny asked. "You really felt the beat. I could tell. I don't think I've ever seen your feet move that fast. Why, it looked like you were hopping across hot coals."

"I thought she was doing the Mexican hat dance," Fiona said. "It looked fun." She started imitating my moves and humming the Mexican hat dance tune.

I groaned, knowing I was never going to hear the end of this.

Beth started inching her way toward the locker room.

"I'm okay, really," I said. "I'll catch up with you later. I have to use the restroom. You know, baby on my bladder, and all." They gave me knowing looks and sly smiles. "Jo and Zoe are over there." I pointed, and the duo clapped their hands, hustling over to say hello while I jogged to the locker room to catch Beth.

Beth had changed her clothes and was just picking up her duffel bag to head out the door in the other direction.

"Beth, I'm so glad I caught you. I never did get to talk to you after the Ladies Auxiliary meeting. I'm really interested in joining."

"You can save the act, Mrs. Stone." Her gaze ran over me in an assessing manner. "Michael already warned me you would be looking for me. He's the guilty one. Not me. I'm the victim here. I'm so embarrassed over the scandal he's caused. I have a child. It's my job to protect him, no matter what."

"I'm pregnant, and I already feel so protective over my child. I can only imagine what you must be going through," I said sincerely. It was so true how quickly feelings could change. Once I got over the shock of being pregnant and the panic of a huge baby and me possibly being a bad mother, the thought of having a baby growing inside me made me fiercely protective all of a sudden.

She relaxed her shoulders a little.

"Your husband claims you were having an affair as well," I added while I still had a chance, "and Cal Stanton claims he is your alibi. That you were with him the night of the murder. Is that true?"

Her body filled with tension once more. "My husband is desperate and willing to say anything, and Cal is a friend who is only trying to protect me. I was with Cal working late on a project together, but that's all. And if you want to know anything else, you can talk to my lawyer."

Beth strode past me with her head held high. I followed but let her leave, wondering why she was still being so secretive. She was hiding something. I could feel it. And I still had no idea what that vision could mean, but one thing was certain.

I wouldn't stop digging until I got to the truth.

I SCROLLED THROUGH THE SOCIAL MEDIA APPS ON MY phone later that morning in our kitchen. Mitch insisted on cooking me breakfast before he left for work. Morty was once again hovering close by. He paced and fussed as he had been for a while now, but I finally attributed it to my pregnancy. My two boys were such worrywarts, but I had to admit, it warmed my heart.

"Oh, no he didn't." I gaped at my phone.

"What?" Mitch asked, looking over my shoulder as he set a plate of eggs, turkey sausage, whole wheat toast and fruit before me.

No hashbrowns in sight.

Stifling the urge to frown, I focused on the question he'd asked me instead. Looking back at my phone, I pointed at the images and videos on the screen.

"Who's that?" He squinted.

"Ginger and Honey Lowenthal."

"Seriously?" His eyes grew wide. "It doesn't even look like them." Mitch sat down and started shoveling forkfuls of eggs, hashbrowns and bacon into his mouth before asking, "I thought they were supposed to be internet sensations."

"Wannabe social media influencers to be exact," I said, "but that was before Danny McMasters doctored their videos and pictures." I took a bite of scrambled eggs and turkey sausage, trying not to drool over his bacon and potatoes. I thought about Danny as a distraction. "He must have saved the originals because these had the really bad parts he'd obviously edited out."

"Why post the originals now?" Mitch asked. "I don't get it. I thought he was helping the twins in exchange for their affection." He snorted. "That's sure not going to win him any favors." He shook his head. "Amateurs."

"Um, I seem to remember someone else who wasn't so smooth when I first came to town," I responded.

"I must have done something right because you chose me instead of Dawson." Mitch waggled his eyebrows at me.

"Good Lord. I didn't even know Dawson was flirting with me."

"Now who's the one who wasn't so smooth?"

I rolled my eyes at him. "Anyway, Danny was trying to help the twins because he thought they really liked him. Something must have happened to make him post these." I cringed as I looked at the pictures and videos on my phone again. "I saw the Lowenthal twins were signed up with a personal trainer this morning. I'm thinking I might have to go back to the gym and catch them while they're still there."

"Wait," Mitch's fork paused halfway to his mouth, "you went to the gym?"

I smacked him on the arm, and he chuckled. "That's all you got out of that?"

"I'm just teasing you, babe." He winked. "I heard all about your stellar Zumba moves from Wally."

"Already? Geesh the grapevine moves fast in Divinity."

"What did you expect? Small town living at its best."

"Was Wally impressed?"

"He was...surprised. Let's just leave it at that." His face sobered. "But, seriously, should you be exercising?"

I gladly ignored both of his comments. "I wonder if the twins will still claim they were with Danny on the night of the murder after this? I have so many questions."

"Speaking of the McMasters. I followed up with Michael's alibi of being at home that night." Mitch sat back and wiped his mouth. "His housekeeper confirmed his story."

"Of course, she did. The woman's no dummy." I pushed the rest of my food away, eyeing the last of my husband's hashbrowns and plotting how I was going to snag them. "I'm sure she knows many of McMasters secrets, but she wants to keep her job."

"Exactly." He turned around to grab his notebook off the counter, then faced me as he flipped through it. He paused. "Where'd the rest of my hashbrown go?"

I pointed at Morty, who just blinked at us with a

piece of straw sticking out of his fur. Every time he came home lately, he dragged some sort of debris into the house.

Mitch glanced at Morty and then studied my face with narrowed eyes. "Next time you might want to wipe the grease off your chin before answering."

I swallowed, trying hard not to moan with pleasure. "I don't know what you're talking about," I finally got out as I took my dishes to the sink and wiped my face only after my back was to him. "Where are you off to today?" I changed the subject.

He brought his dishes to the sink, nudged me out of the way, and proceeded to clean up. The man literally wouldn't let me lift a finger. It drove me crazy. My pregnancy wasn't a handicap. I was perfectly capable of doing things for myself. I grabbed the dishcloth and wiped off the table.

"I have an appointment with Rita Haynes and her lawyer to finally question her." He took the dishcloth from me and dried the table.

"Okay, good." I grabbed my purse off counter.

"The fact that you didn't ask to go with me has me worried."

"I have a couple clients today." I hesitated a moment before adding, "I'm being honest with you like you asked me to, so you can't get mad. First, I'm going to try to talk to the twins at the gym. Nothing scary or dangerous, I promise. I've had my fill of exercise."

A muscle in his jaw bulged, but all he said was, "Let me know how it goes."

"That's it?" My mouth fell open. "What's the catch?"

"No catch. That's it." He rubbed a hand over his whiskered jaw. "I'm trying to back off a little like you asked me to."

"Okay then." I nodded once and smiled.

He grabbed his badge and gun and headed for the door.

"Mitch?"

He stopped and looked over his shoulder.

"I love you, husband."

His whole face softened as he strode over to me, planted a firm kiss on my lips, then walked out the door with purposeful strides saying, "I love you too, wife. Now let me go before I change my mind."

And then he was gone.

16

I hurried back to Walley's World, hoping I didn't miss the twins. I walked into the gym, straight to the front desk.

Walley actually took a step back, eying me warily. "I can't believe my eyes. Mrs. Stone in the flesh. Haven't you been Walley-sized enough for one day?"

"Trust me, I have no intention of working out possibly ever again."

He frowned. "Then what are you doing here?"

I pointed into the weight room of the gym. "I'm here on official business. I need to question the Lowenthal twins about the investigation, but I promise I won't be a disruption for your members."

"The moment you walked through my doors, you became a disruption to my members. I do believe many are traumatized enough from this morning's class."

"What if I promise never to come back?"

"Deal. Just make it quick."

"Thank you." I hurried past the exercise class rooms and headed into the weight room, staying in the corner as I scanned the area as discreetly as I could.

I spotted the twins immediately. They were made up perfectly as usual, wearing the latest fashion in athletic wear. They were both on weightlifting machines, and a man who looked as though he had just stepped off of the cover of Muscle Magazine was instructing them on the proper techniques. They hung on his every word, looking ready to drool at any moment, no cell phones in sight.

Clearly, they hadn't seen the videos.

Hearing a commotion, I glanced out of the room toward the front door. "Oh, boy, this isn't going to end well," I said out loud, watching the man of the hour slip past the front desk and make a bee line toward the girls.

Danny McMasters' face darkened to nearly purple as he marched toward them, pushing up his glasses along the way. He came to a stop in front of the three of them and balled his hands into fists.

"What do you think you're doing," he said, glaring at the three of them.

"Who are you?" Muscle Man looked over Danny's scrawny frame. "Cuz you definitely don't belong in here, dude."

"Oh, my gosh, Danny what are you doing here?" Ginger glanced around nervously. "You're not supposed to be in here."

"Yeah, you need to leave like now," Honey added.

"Is that why you came here? Because you knew I normally wouldn't step foot in a gym? I knew you were avoiding me for a reason. You'll understand why I had to punish you for cheating on me with this muscle head, but I can forgive you if you leave with me now and never do this again. You're *my* girls," Danny said. "Let's bail."

"Stop saying that," Ginger hissed. "We're not your girls."

"Yeah, we're not your anything," Honey replied, then turned to Muscle Man. "We're so sorry about this. Don't pay any attention to him. He's nobody."

"Nobody?" Danny gaped at them both, looking hurt and confused. "How can you say that? After everything I did for you both. I thought I meant something to you."

"You were a means to an end, Danny," Ginger said.

"Nothing more," Honey added. "Definitely nothing more. You can't honestly think you are in our league."

"So, that's it? You're done with me?"

"Yes, I mean, how many times do we have to say it?" Honey said, laughing and rolling her eyes.

"Seriously," Ginger added with an exaggerated shudder. "You can go now. You're embarrassing us."

"I can't believe this is happening." Danny clenched his jaw and straightened his spine. "You think I'm nobody, but you forget my last name. I was willing to make things right, but not now. You're going to be sorry. I can promise you that." He turned around and stormed out of the gym.

"What is he talking about?" Honey asked.

"Who knows," Ginger replied, and the girls continued their training session, having no idea their world was about to change in a big way.

I would deal with them later. Right now, I had a bigger fish to catch, I thought as I hurried after him.

"Danny, wait up." I came to a stop beside him, out of breath after my short jog.

He scowled. "What do you want?"

"I know you were protecting them before. But after

that little show, you have no reason to protect them anymore."

He hesitated, looked back at the gym with a mixture of hurt and anger, then responded, "You're right. You're absolutely right."

"What does that mean?"

"Ginger and Honey no longer have an alibi."

"So, to be completely clear, you're admitting you weren't with the Lowenthal twins the night of Audra's murder?"

"No, but now I can guess who was." He glared toward the gym.

"Then can I ask where you were?"

He faced me again. "I was at home. My housekeeper can verify everything."

I bet she could, but then again, she would probably say anything to keep her job.

"You were with your father then?"

Danny's face hardened even more than moments ago in the gym. "I wasn't with my father. I'm never with my father, and don't want to be." His voice took on a tone filled with animosity as he added, "Frankly, Mrs. Stone, he deserves everything that's coming to him," whatever that meant, and then he walked away.

LATER THAT AFTERNOON, I WALKED INTO SMOKEY JO'S Tavern and sat at the bar. Jo set a glass of milk with veggies and hummus in front of me.

"Awww, come on. Not you too," I said.

"That's right, me too, missy," she said loudly, looking around most likely for my husband. After a moment, she set a basket of cheese fries in front of me with a caffeine-free soda. "Leave the milk and veggies out in case any of your family comes in. If you're caught, I know nothing. You stole the fries from the back. That's my story, and I'm sticking to it." She disappeared into the kitchen.

"You are a goddess," I hollered after her as I stuck a fry in my mouth and moaned in ecstasy between chews, my eyes rolling back. Nothing had ever tasted better. I felt like I was doing something illegal. I kept guarding my plate, my gaze darting around the room, daring anyone to try and take my goodies away.

"And *you* are busted," said a man's voice from behind me.

I turned around, feeling the heat all the way to my ears. "Hi Doc."

He sat down beside me. "I won't tell my wife, if you don't tell her I stopped in for some of Jo's peach cobbler. She's got me on this no dessert kick, watching my cholesterol. Trust me when I say I feel your pain."

I let out a huge sigh of relief. "You've got a deal."

Jo brought out the doctor's dessert without him even having to ask and then looked at us both with condemnation. "Listen, you two. I'm all for the extra business, but I can't keep being your dealers, 'kay? Next time I'm gonna need partner consent."

"Fine," we both mumbled at the same time and then laughed.

At that moment, the Lowenthal twins walked in and sat in the far corner. Several eyes looked their way and the room filled with whispers. I couldn't believe my luck and wasn't about to pass up this opportunity to talk to the girls.

"Thanks, Jo." I set money on the bar for both our treats. "See ya, Doc. I've got something I need to do. Enjoy your last meal."

"Much obliged, Sunny." He raised his fork. "I'm savoring every bite."

I walked over to the booth the twins sat in with their heads bent close together. They didn't even notice me at first. I cleared my throat, and they jerked apart.

"Oh, it's you," Ginger said.

"What do you want?" Honey asked, looking at me with weary, red-rimmed eyes. It was clear she'd been crying.

"May I sit down?"

"Do we have a choice?" Ginger asked.

I sat without answering. "I know it must be difficult living in a small town with those videos circulating."

"You have no idea," Honey said, sniffling. "We're so embarrassed. He came into the gym, knowing what he had done, and actually expected us to ever forgive him? He's out of his mind."

"*You're* embarrassed," Ginger said, dry eyed. "*I'm* pissed. That little twerp is gonna pay for this."

"Don't you think that's why he did it in the first place?" I asked gently, trying to put my mother's hat on and give them some useful advice. "He was pretty upset himself after he left the gym earlier."

"He doesn't even belong to the gym, so he shouldn't even have been there." Honey blew her nose with a tissue. "He never would have seen anything if he'd done what he was told and played by the rules."

"That's beside the point." I gave up on being motherly and put my investigator hat on instead as I studied them both. "The fact is, he *was* there, and you two embarrassed him in front of a lot of people."

"So," Ginger said with a shrug. "He doesn't mean anything to us. Why should we care how he feels?"

"He *should* mean something to you. It's pretty clear from the original videos that he did a lot for you both. Maybe if you had been a little more grateful and nicer, he wouldn't have felt the need to get back at you." These girls were unbelievable. Good Lord, I hoped my own kids wouldn't turn out like this. "I don't understand why it's so important to you to be famous if it's all fake anyway."

"We don't need a lecture from you," Ginger said. "We already got a big one from our parents." Well, that was good to hear at least.

"No, she's right, Ginger," Honey said. "We were so mean to Danny. All he ever did was try to help us with everything we asked of him."

"We can't help it he got the wrong idea," Ginger said.

"I think you could help it," I replied. "You didn't have to lead him on. Some people can't handle that kind of attention."

"Yeah, that's pretty clear now. He went way beyond liking us. He became possessive. Like, he actually thought we were his, and he could do whatever he wanted with us," Ginger pointed out, and Honey shuddered.

"That does sound disturbing." I made a note in my notebook. "Look, I'm not trying to lecture you girls. Trust me, I grew up getting plenty of lectures myself and hated every minute of it."

Ginger relaxed in her seat, Honey tilted her head, and both girls looked me in the eyes with genuine interest now.

"I know Audra gave you a confusing reading. She could have been much clearer and advised you better. I also know you lied about being with Danny the night she was murdered. He says he went home and his story checks out." I'd followed up on a few things this morning after I talked with Danny. Turns out his dad was also at home, but Danny obviously wanted nothing to do with him.

"We were with Biff Bickerson all night," Ginger said. "Ask him. He'll tell you the same thing."

"Danny suggested you might use Biff as your alibi. I already talked to him." I winced. "I'm sorry, girls, to have to tell you this, but Biff said he was at the gym training alone. Wally verified he left the gym open that night for Biff to train after hours for his upcoming bodybuilding competition. The cameras show neither of you were there that night."

Honey started crying all over again, her perfectly made-up plastic face melting. While Ginger's face hardened into a glare.

"I'm just trying to help you girls. These are all questions the police are going to ask you. If you don't have an alibi and you do have motive, then you could find yourselves actual suspects in a murder case. Is that what you want?"

"No." Ginger hung her head, blinking back tears of her own.

"We hated Audra for taking our money, knowing we were going to fail," Honey said, "but we're not murderers. We're teenagers."

"I believe you," I said and meant it. They were a hot mess for sure, but I wasn't sensing any dangerous vibes from them. "Why don't you start by telling me the truth, and I will see what I can do to help."

"Okay, we'll tell you everything," Ginger said, adding, "but the first person you should talk to is our therapist."

"Rita Haynes?" I asked. "She said you left her and went to Audra for help."

"And that is the biggest lie of all. We had no choice but to turn to Audra."

"Why?"

"Because Rita Haynes is a fraud. None of her clients left her. She kicked us all out and locked herself in her office. For someone who helps crazy people, she turned out to be the craziest person of all."

17

The stress of this case was taking its toll on me. I headed to Cindy Mallone's massage parlor for some much-needed relief. Cindy and Gary from Gary's Hardware had finally started dating. She'd invested in his business to help him expand and had become a partner in more ways than one. They both decided to take a chance on love and were happier than ever. Cindy and I had grown close after I'd helped fix them up. Gary was one of my usual customers, living his life by his horoscope.

I walked inside the massage parlor. Soft meditation music filtered through the sound system, relaxing me instantly. The walls were painted a calming pale blue, the waiting room chairs soft and inviting. Lemon and orange water, as well as cucumber water, sat invitingly on a table off to the side, along with warm fingertip towels.

Cindy's secretary, Amy, sat behind the front desk, her slicked-back gray hair looking chic as usual. She looked up and smiled. "Hi, Mrs. Stone. Cindy is with a customer, but you can go get ready in the next room. She'll be with you in a minute."

"Thanks, Amy." I wandered down the hall when I

spotted Cindy coming out of her office, getting ready to enter a room. She was a petite woman with pink hair and pale bluish-purple eyes.

"Hi, Sunny." She smiled wide when she spotted me. "I'll be right with you. I'm almost done with this client." She looked around the empty hallway and lowered her voice. "Poor guy was Audra Grimshaw's boyfriend. No wonder he's so tense."

"You're giving Greg Gates a massage?" This day was turning out to be quite an enlightening one.

"Yes, why?"

"Would you mind if I asked him a few questions before you finish?" I put my hands together in a prayer position.

"I don't know about that, Sunny." Her face puckered into one of concentration before finally responding, "I'm a professional, and this is my place of business. This could ruin my reputation."

"I know." I dropped my hands. "I totally understand if it's a no. It's just hard to pin this guy down. I only need a few minutes, I promise."

"Well," she chewed her bottom lip then added, "I do owe you for helping me with Gary. He never would have taken a chance on us if it wasn't for you. Just this once, I'll allow it. You've got five minutes."

"Thank you so much." I slipped into the room before she could change her mind and shut the door behind me.

What Cindy didn't know is that Gary would never answer my questions if he knew it was me. So, I kept the lights low and disguised my voice, pretending to be Cindy. We were both petite.

How hard could it be?

"Relax your body, Mr. Gates. Your muscles are so tense." I squeezed his neck and shoulder muscles.

Grabbing some essential oil, I poured on way too much. Wincing, I rubbed the oil in as I worked the muscles, not having a clue what I was doing. "I was sorry to hear about your girlfriend. That had to be difficult for you."

"It was difficult for sure, but Audra brought this on herself. She made a lot of enemies over the past several months. She changed after coming to Divinity." He flinched and started to squirm. "What are you doing? That tickles. Do you actually know what you're doing? I heard good things about this place, but now I'm not so sure."

"Sorry, I was trying a new technique." I stopped strumming my fingertips over his ribs as if I were playing Beethoven's 5th. I balled my hands into fists, digging my knuckles into various spots across his back with occasional slaps in between like Granny Gert had taught me when kneading dough. For the life of me, I couldn't remember the way Cindy did my massages, so I was improvising.

"Just give me the normal massage," he muttered, shifting his position on the table as if he were uncomfortable.

I started karate chopping his spine, then waxing on and off in true Karate Kid fashion. "Audra mentioned to me that someone kept texting her and wouldn't leave her alone. It scared her," I said, hoping to distract him from my amateur technique. He had to wonder where I'd gotten my training.

"It's public knowledge that she admitted having an affair with Michael McMasters in her diary. My guess is it's one of them who was harassing her. Why so many questions?" He started to sit up, but I slapped a hot towel on his back. He let out an expletive then relaxed on a sigh, sinking into the table.

Hmmm, must be I did something right. "I see you're moving on already. Word around town is that you and Willow Goodbody are a thing."

He stiffened, then rolled over, pulling the sheet with him as he sat up.

Whoops.

I had to look up at him. I'd forgotten how big the man was. I swallowed when he narrowed his eyes, the first shiver of real fear trickling through me.

"You're not Cindy Mallone."

"No...no, I'm." I took a step back. "Were you and Willow a thing already on the night of Audra's murder?"

"No, we weren't." He clenched his jaw. "Look, I'm the victim here. Audra cheated on me months before the Psychic Fair. She got pregnant with another man's child. I have every right to be angry and to move on with whomever I want."

"Yes, yes you do. And you also have a motive for wanting Audra dead." I moved closer to the door.

He stood, and the sheet wrapped around his torso fell to the floor. "Now, who's the one harassing people, Mrs. Stone?"

"I'm not harassing anyone." I kept my eyes firmly locked on his face and put my hand on the doorknob. "I'm interning because I might add massages to my services."

He grunted as he picked up his sheet and wrapped it around his waist again, thank goodness. "Don't quit your day job." He took a step toward me, and my relief was short lived. "Let me pound on your back for a while, and I'll show you what it feels like to have someone *intern* on your body. Last I checked you were supposed to be licensed."

"You're so right. My bad. Speaking of my day job,

I've got to run." I slipped out the door, closing it firmly behind me. "He's all yours. I warmed him up for you," I said to Cindy as I passed her.

"Sunny Stone, you were only supposed to *talk* to him." Cindy put her hands on her hips. "What did you do?"

"Just a little wax on, wax off, paint the fence." I demonstrated the moves. "You know, massage techniques."

"Okay, Mr. Miyagi, you've seen one too many movies." She laughed. "Let's let the professional take it from here, but just so you know, I'm claiming I had no idea you snuck into his room and pretended to be me."

"That's fair," I said, adding, "You can gladly take over. Careful with that one. He's got anger issues. I wouldn't want him taking out his frustrations over me on you." I looked at the door, and an uneasy feeling settled in my gut.

"Oh, honey, I'm a ninth-degree black belt. You can't get any higher than that. He won't want to be getting angry with me, but thanks for the warning."

"You're welcome, and thank you for letting me question him. I know you weren't comfortable with that, so I really appreciate it all the more."

"I hope you got what you wanted because it won't happen again. We're even now," she said before heading into his room.

I might not have gotten the answers to my questions from Greg's mouth, but the stamp on his hand told me all I needed to know.

"This is crazy, Tink, you can't dance." Mitch held my hand as we walked into the Song Bird with Jo and Cole.

The Song Bird was a Japanese karaoke bar on the edge of town.

"She sure can't," Jo said above the loud music coming from the stage, trying not to laugh but failing miserably.

"She can't sing, either," Cole added with a deep belly laugh, not trying to hide his amusement in the least.

"Hey, *she* is standing right here." I dropped Mitch's hand and crossed my arms, staring at all three of them. This brought back memories of when I first met Cole in this very bar. He'd changed so much since back then.

"I mean you can't dance because you're pregnant, babe," Mitch clarified as if that were any better.

I threw up my hands, letting out an exasperated sound, then headed for the bar. "I'm going to get a drink." I pointed a finger in Mitch's face. "A Shirley Temple and a handful of peanuts. And if I see a vegetable of any kind anywhere near me, someone's gonna get hurt. Just sayin'."

They followed me without another word.

A short time later we found an open table in the corner and sat down, catching up with conversation. Cole took a turn at singing, amazing the crowd as usual with his silky deep baritone voice. He had an incredible gift. I'd often told him he needed to try out for a reality singing competition, but he liked his life just the way it was. Simple and full of love. Jo danced in front of the stage with stars in her eyes. That was enough for him.

"You're not much for karaoke," my husband said,

studying me as I kept scanning the room. "Why tonight?"

My gaze landed on the door, and I grinned in satisfaction as I pointed in that direction. "That's why."

In walked Greg Gates and Willow Goodbody.

"How'd you know they would be here?" Mitch asked, looking impressed and a little suspicious.

"A little birdie told me." I wasn't giving away all my secrets in case this was another test from my detective husband.

"Haha, but seriously." His eyes became slits. "How?"

"Let's just say I followed the signs, Detective Grumpy Pants."

He let that go, most likely thinking I was talking about psychic signs. But my over protective husband didn't need to know about that little tidbit. He'd never let me out of his sight again.

Willow headed to the bathroom while Greg made a beeline for the bar.

"You thinking what I'm thinking, Tink?" Mitch asked, transforming into in full detective mode now.

"Divide and conquer," I responded, already standing up.

I walked into the bathroom and looked under the stalls. No one else was in there except Willow and myself. I waited by the mirror.

"I'll be out in a minute, Mrs. Stone," Willow said.

There was no way she could have seen me come in, but then again, she was a psychic as well. I sometimes forgot I wasn't the only one in town now. Moments later, Willow emerged from the stall and washed her hands.

"The answer is, yes, I am here with Greg, but you

already knew that. Ask me what you really want to know."

"Okay, Ms. Goodbody, why did you say you were with Dawson the night of Audra's murder?" I watched her closely.

"Because I was." She shrugged. "I have nothing to hide."

"But we both know you didn't go to his place until one in the morning." I studied her body language. "Were you with Greg Gates before that?"

She laughed. "Don't get me wrong. I like men, yes, but not two in the same night." She wrinkled up her nose.

"Then where were you after the storm hit until one a.m.?"

"I was at the Psychic Fair in my tent still."

"Why? Everyone left."

"Not everyone."

I pulled out my handy dandy notebook that I always carried with me. "So, you weren't alone?"

"No."

I looked up at her. "Who were you with?"

"I can't tell you." She applied more lipstick in the mirror.

"Can't or won't?"

"Definitely can't." She made eye contact in the glass. "You more than anyone should know about psychic client confidentiality." She dropped her lipstick back in her purse and faced me. "You're looking in the wrong direction, Mrs. Stone. I'm not the one you need to be questioning."

"Someone came to you for a reading but doesn't want anyone to know." The wheels in my brain were turning with possibilities.

"Correct. And that's all I'm going to say about that.

You have a good evening now. I'm going to go try to salvage what's left of mine after you and your husband put a damper on it." She left, and I was impressed once more that she could see Mitch was questioning Greg.

Her ability was strong.

It dawned on me if the killer was another psychic, I might have just met my match.

18

I walked into Divine Inspiration the next afternoon and saw Olivia Ventura having tea with my mother.

"Hi, Mrs. Stone, it's lovely to see you again," Sally Clark the housekeeper said to me.

I'd been coming around more often since my mother and I had our talk and put our past behind us. That, and the Tasty Trio was giving me cooking lessons. "Awww, thanks, Ms. Clark. It's so nice to see more of you as well."

"How are you feeling?"

"I'm doing okay. The morning sickness is getting better finally, thank goodness. Great-Grandma Tootsie gave me an herbal tea that really helps."

"That's wonderful. We're all pretty excited around here to hear the patter of little feet. It's been far too long." Sally had worked at the inn for the better half of her life. She'd stayed on after the former innkeeper was murdered and my parents took over. My mother certainly wouldn't have been able to run the place without her.

Little feet. I swallowed hard then pasted on a smile, not yet ready to think about how those little feet, which might not be so little, were going to arrive. "Oh, my mother spotted me." I waved. "I'd better get on in there. Take care, Ms. Clark."

"You too, dear."

I walked into the living room and joined the women, taking the chair next to my mother. "Hi, ladies. How are you both?"

"I'm a mess of nerves, considering there's a murderer still running around on the loose in our sweet town." Olivia's hand fluttered to her chest. "It's just awful that the police haven't caught the killer yet. I don't know what's taking so long. I don't feel safe walking around Divinity alone."

"I know what you mean." My mother fanned her face. "Why, it gives me the vapors thinking that I could be talking to the killer and not even know it. It could be anyone in town, and half of them are staying at my inn. So many people were at that Psychic Fair. You would think with all the psychics, someone would know something."

I looked at my mother and realized she believe in psychic ability more than she let on. "That's true, and I promise you I will get to the bottom of this," I said, "but I don't want you ladies to worry. Detective Stone and the rest of the police department are hard at work on solving this case. They'll make sure the streets of Divinity are safe. Not to mention, poor Sean O'Malley is a mess being the prime suspect. Everyone knows Sean. There's no way he's the real killer."

"I, for one, don't know Mr. O'Malley all that well," Olivia said. "He doesn't exactly travel in our circles, does he, Vivian?"

"No," my mother admitted, "no he doesn't. But I *do* know Sean, and I can vouch for him. He's a good man."

"Well, I'm not taking any chances, and you shouldn't either." Olivia sipped her tea daintily then addressed me. "I've convinced your mother to take Wally's strength training class with me. I've been going for a year now and have seen a big difference. A woman needs to know how to defend herself in to-day's world, and yoga isn't going to cut it."

"That's not a bad idea, Mom. Maybe I'll join you."

"Sorry, darling, but I'm pretty sure Wally banned you from the gym. Too much trouble happens when you're around." She patted my hand.

"Story of my life." I shook my head. "Where's Dad?"

"Don't even get me started. He's out back with Harold, of course, but now they've lured poor Antonio into fishing with them. It's not even dusk. They're not going to catch anything, but you can't tell those men anything. Even Frank tried to tell them, but they didn't care one bit."

Frank LaLone was the maintenance man who also stayed on when my parents took over. He helped the men with maintenance issues as well as keeping up the grounds. If it wasn't for Sally and Frank staying on, the inn never would have been successful in its re-opening.

"Oh, I don't mind," Olivia said. "My Tony is so worried about the horse races; he needs to destress any way he can. Let him fish." She tsked and shook her head. "Maybe then he'll stop complaining to me."

Morty came into the room with a piece of paper in his mouth.

I reached down and took it from him. "Look, it's a betting slip from Saratoga. Maybe it's a sign Sweet Life will win his next race," I said.

"He'd better start winning something, or he won't

have a stable to come back to," Olivia muttered, then frowned. "If only Rich Hastings would stay away from Mark. He's distracting him to the point where Mark can't focus on his job as a vet like he's paid to do. I don't trust Rich one bit."

Rich did claim that Mark was his alibi and Mark verified that, but Zoe had proof that his alibi was a lie. Why was Mark lying for Rich Hastings? And where had Rich really gone that night? I still had so many questions, but the information was privileged since the case was still ongoing, so I kept the knowledge to myself. It did, however, remind me to follow up with Mark. There had to be an explanation.

Great-Grandma Tootsie brought out another pot of tea and scones. "Here you are, ladies. Enjoy."

Morty stared at me for a long moment, then followed Toots into the kitchen. I knew he was trying to tell me something, but, as usual, I hadn't figured out what yet. Staring down at the betting slip, I decided maybe that follow-up with Mark would happen sooner rather than later. Finishing my tea, I hugged my mother and bid my farewells.

Maybe it was time I did a little wagering myself.

DOLCE VITA STABLES WAS IMPRESSIVE. HORSE RACING thoroughbred horses started with a strategy that began years before planning a mating and making a purchase. The Ventura family had been known as one of the best stables to produce winning horses for centuries. I understood the pressure for Antonio to continue the legacy. It didn't sound like he was a good businessman with the bad investments he'd made. Add to that a horse that was on a losing streak, and a queen of high society wife with expensive tastes like my mother. It was understandable why he seemed so stressed out.

I'd done my research. Sweet Life was two and would hit his stride at three. The other horses were only one and not ready to compete yet. The older horses didn't race anymore but were still useful as studs. But if a horse started to lose, he wouldn't be useful for anything other than the glue factory. It cost too much money to feed a horse that wasn't useful.

Poor Sweet Life. I had a feeling the stallion's days were numbered.

I walked around, trying to pay attention to details like my detective husband would, and taking in my surroundings with a critical eye. The grounds consisted of a training center, as well as a rehabilitation center and gorgeous barns the horses slept and ate in. There were employees scattered around the grounds completing various tasks, though I had a feeling there were a few less than normal given the money issues.

A feeling in my gut pulled me toward one barn in particular on the edge of the property. I heard voices as I drew closer. Familiar voices. Slipping inside as quietly as I could, I ducked into an empty stall and peeked through a crack.

"I don't care what anyone says, you need to stick to the story. I was with you the night of Audra's murder. We talked about racing and had drinks and I spent the night at your place," Rich Hastings said to Mark Silverman. "Got it?"

"It's too late," Mark replied, pacing around the barn, looking as agitated as Morty lately. "Zoe told me that she told Sunny Stone that we facetimed that evening for hours and I was alone. Sunny is not stupid, Rich."

"She might be married to a detective, but she's not a real detective herself. And do you honestly believe she's psychic?" He made a set of air quotes. "You need to relax, man. Just chill before you blow us both in. What Zoe said doesn't mean anything, dude." Rich kicked a pile of hay as he walked past it. "Just because she didn't see me, doesn't mean I wasn't there. I mean, I could have been in another room for all she knew."

"Come on, man. Listen to how ridiculous you sound. Why would you stay if I was on my phone with Zoe?" Mark scrubbed a hand through his perfectly styled blond hair, making it look as messy as their alibi. "Your whole story was that we were drinking together and talking about the racing season. It wouldn't make sense for you to be at my place just sitting here, drinking alone, waiting for me to get off the phone. No one is going to buy that."

"I don't know. You're confusing me." Rich paced, running his hands over his bald head and then down over his thick dark beard. "You're making this way more complicated than it has to be. Look, it doesn't really matter if it makes sense. Just stick to the story. If we both stick to the same story, then they can't prove anything."

"I don't know, man." Mark shook his head. "I don't like this. It's getting too complicated."

"You stick to the story, or I'll tell everyone what we've really been doing together." Rich handed Mark an envelope. "We've got a good thing going here. Don't blow this by suddenly growing a conscience."

Mark stopped walking and took the envelope but didn't say anything as he watched Rich leave the barn. Sweet Life whinnied, and Mark ran a hand over the horse's nose. "I know, pal. I don't like it either, but what choice do I have?"

"You have only one choice," I said as I stepped out of the stall.

Mark jumped, stumbling back and grabbing his chest. "I think I lost ten years of my life, thank you very much."

"Yeah, well I'm not about to let Sean O'Malley lose ten years of his life or more because you won't tell the truth."

Mark looked down at the envelope he clutched in his hands. "I don't know what you're talking about."

"I HEARD EVERYTHING. YOU MAY AS WELL TELL ME WHAT that conversation with Rich Hastings means, or I'll be forced to draw my own conclusions and tell my husband. Is that really what you want?"

"Look, I'm a vet and a damn good one." He held his head high, sounding more like he was trying to prove that to himself than me.

"I don't deny that. Zoe and Jo wouldn't vouch for you if you weren't a good man." I stared at him for a long moment. "I don't know what kind of trouble you got yourself mixed up in, but murder is never okay. I know you don't like Sean, but how can you do this to Zoe? You say you love her, but this is not the way to show it. She'll never forgive you if she finds out you had a part in her fiancé going to jail for a murder he didn't commit." Nothing else I could have said would sway Mark, but the mention of Zoe had his walls crumbling. I actually felt sorry for the man. It was clear he still loved her.

He let out a huge breath, then his shoulders slumped as he admitted, "I met Rich years ago when I first became a vet. We both liked to gamble, and the rush of winning was thrilling." He met my eyes. "A little too thrilling."

"I gathered maybe he had a problem with gambling, but you too?"

Mark nodded. "So much so, I wagered everything I have, including this practice, to the wrong sort of people."

"I'm listening."

"The sort of people who break your legs or worse if you don't pay. So, I had to find a way to start winning."

"How can you be certain of winning? It's a gamble with every bet."

He looked me in the eye as he admitted, "Not when you form an alliance with the right people where everyone wins."

A knot formed in my gut. "What did you do?"

"Nothing like murder, I promise you." He held up his hands. "I gave inside information on certain horses and their weaknesses. We knew what ones were beatable. We also knew which jockeys were willing to throw a race. All of this inside information determined who we would bet on each race."

"And the people who ran the bets never caught on?" This didn't seem plausible, given how big thoroughbred racing was and the stakes involved and millions of dollars placed on who would win.

Mark's face flushed, and he looked down at his feet, not able to meet my gaze. "Our bets didn't take place legally."

"I don't understand."

He looked around as if to be sure we were alone before finally meeting my eyes. "We were part of an underground illegal gambling ring with high stakes players."

I gasped. "Isn't that dangerous?"

"Very if I get caught." Mark undid a button on his lab coat. "Not to mention career damaging if the horse racing circle found out about it. No one would allow me to be their vet anymore, and all the people I swindled would most definitely want me dead."

I'd always trusted my gut, and my gut was twisting in knots at the moment. "Rich Hastings is blackmailing you, isn't he?"

Mark's mouth fell open. "I don't care what anyone says, you're the real deal." He nodded, his eyes filling up with moisture. "I've let so many people down. Mr. Ventura and Zoe. All the people I care about."

"Maybe you can make amends for that now," I said, waiting until he looked at me before I continued. "Where was Rich the night of the murder?"

"I honestly don't know." He looked so ashamed and lost. "I wish I knew, and that's the truth."

"I believe you, Mark. But you need to stop this activity now, or I will have to tell the authorities. Do I make myself clear?"

"Crystal." He let out a huge sigh. "This is actually a relief because I couldn't stomach living this way anymore."

I nodded. "Be careful, Mark. It sounds like these people aren't ones to be taken lightly. I would hate to see anything bad happen to you."

"I will, but I'm not half as worried about myself as I am you, Sunny." His gaze met mine intensely. "There's still a killer out there somewhere. A killer who won't like you getting closer to the truth."

A gust of wind swept through the barn, swirling up hay and dust, and I had the strongest premonition his words were about to come true. I nodded my thanks and headed outside to my car. A chill crept up my spine, and suddenly I felt eyes on me. I had a strange sensation that I had been here before or knew someone who had. Maybe it had something to do with Granny Gert. Helga had said my grandmother was psychic back in the day; she just hadn't honed her craft. I'd have to have another talk with my grandmother. There was definitely more to her story than she was telling me.

I reached my car, and goosebumps slithered up my spine. Whipping around, I let out a little scream.

"Morty!" I reached down and picked him up. "Don't scare me like that ever again. I get it. I know what you were trying to tell me with the betting slip, and you were right. Dr. Mark Silverman isn't as perfect as his Ken doll image led people to believe. Let's go, buddy. Daddy's waiting for us at home."

Morty hissed at me then leapt out of my arms and disappeared.

"Sorry, Mitch. I tried." Maybe Mark was right, and Morty was feeling left out with the new baby. But how could I reassure him if he was never around? Hopefully, my husband would have better luck with our human baby. Hopefully we both would. Because at the moment, our future with our fur baby wasn't looking too bright.

19

The stables were on the outskirts of town, probably twenty minutes from my house. It was summer so the sun didn't set until later, but the rumbling in my stomach told me it was near dinner time. All I could think about was food lately.

I hoped Mitch would have dinner ready when I got there.

I checked my cell, but it was dead. And, of course, I didn't have a charger in my little VW Bug. My detective husband was probably going to put me on lockdown after this.

The sky grew cloudy and dark, heavy with rain about to fall. I started driving and had made it about ten minutes when I noticed the low tire pressure gauge come on. I frowned. I knew Dawson had checked the tire pressure when he fixed it recently. I watched the pressure slowly decrease as I kept driving. Pulling over, I shut the car off. Dawson and Big Don would kill me if I ruined my rims.

Maybe I had driven over something and punctured the tire. Of course, the clouds chose this moment to open up and release a torrential downpour. I didn't have an umbrella handy, either. I climbed out of my car, soaked to the bone instantly as I looked at all of my tires. The back passenger side tire was cut. I was no expert, but even I could tell this wasn't a puncture. It looked like a definite slice, like someone had purposefully cut my tire. I slowly stood and looked around.

Why would anyone do that?

Mark's words came back to haunt me. A killer was still on the loose, and I was getting closer to the truth. I couldn't drive my car, my cell phone was dead, and Morty wasn't with me. This was not good. I saw headlights coming from way down the road. I was about to flag the person down, but they picked up speed. They were coming right at my Bug.

Something made me duck into the woods and hide.

My jaw fell open as I stared in horror. They slammed into the back of my car, pushing it over the edge of the road and into the ditch. My poor Bug didn't stand a chance. It rolled over onto its hood. I shivered, even though it was still in the eighties outside. I could have been inside the car when it rolled. That hit had been deliberate. No one in this area had a white VW Bug with orange, yellow, and pink flowers on the sides. Whoever was behind the wheel of that car wanted to hurt me.

Or worse, wanted me dead.

Brake lights came on from down the road, and the car started backing up. My heartbeat started to pound. They weren't finished with me yet. I turned and headed deeper into the woods, my shorts and t-shirt no match against the mosquitos. I had flip-flops on my bare feet, which hindered my hike over the uneven ground full of pine needles, downed branches, pinecones, and exposed tree roots. The woods blocked out what little light there was, and I had no idea what direction to go in. I just knew my life depended on keeping my feet moving.

So that's what I did.

All I could hope for was that I would be late to dinner. Mitch would definitely know something was wrong if that happened and come looking for me. Except, stupid me hadn't told anyone where I was going. I had so much to learn before becoming a mother. Good lord, I couldn't even take care of myself. How was I supposed to be able to take care of a baby? I could only hope Morty would somehow guide Mitch in my direction, since he had been at the stables with me.

It certainly wouldn't be the first time he'd come to my rescue.

In the meantime, I had to focus on staying alive. The woods were a good ten degrees colder beneath the thick canopy of trees. I heard a sound behind me like footsteps. Although, these woods housed deer and bears and wolves. I shook off those terrifying thoughts and kept moving deeper into the woods with no idea what direction I was traveling in.

The footsteps sounded closer, so I picked up the pace. I started running and didn't stop for what felt like hours: a miserable experience for someone who hated to exercise. I stopped to catch my breath and listen. The footsteps were gone, thank goodness, but I seriously had no idea where I was. I came upon a creak and remembered reading somewhere that creaks lead to rivers and rivers lead to towns. So, I followed the creek and hoped for the best.

Hours later, I finally ran into a river. I was pretty sure it was the one that ran behind Divine Inspiration. I only hoped I was following it in the right direction.

Trudging along the edge, I rolled my ankle and dropped to the ground in pain. After I was done having a serious pity party, I struggled to me feet and limped along.

It had to be late now. The sun had set fully, and I was freezing from being wet. I saw a cave, so I decided I needed shelter for the night. I didn't want to think about what might be living in there, so I picked up a couple of rocks and banged them together before I got to the opening. Something scurried by me, and I screamed. When I was certain no other sounds were coming from inside the cave, I limped into the opening.

If I made it out of this alive, I was going to take a crash course in being a survivalist. I had no idea how to make a fire or gather food. I never thought I'd say this, but I would gladly eat vegetables right here and now. I hovered at the edge of the cave, just far enough inside to get dry, then I curled in a ball on the floor and tried to get warm.

It wasn't long before I fell asleep. I dreamt of two babies again. Granny Gert was chanting something while Helga was throwing stones and reading them. There were people everywhere, and Morty was leading the way like a bloodhound. My cheek felt wet. I swiped away my tears, then felt the wetness again. Something licked me.

I bolted up into a sitting position and screamed.

Morty blinked at me.

I cried in relief as I scooped him up and kissed his head.

"Tink, where are you? Please answer me, baby," I heard a deep voice call out.

My heart melted. "I-In here," I managed to get out. "I'm in the cave with Morty."

Moments later, Mitch appeared in the entrance. "Oh, thank God." He dropped to his knees and inspected every inch of me. "Are you hurt?"

"Just my ankle. I think I sprained it." I started crying again. "I'm so glad you found me. Do you have a snack?"

Mitch's face finally softened, and he chuckled. "No, babe, I don't. But when we get home, you can have anything you want."

"E-Even fries?"

"With cheese," he answered and scooped me up into his arms. He stood and walked out of the cave into the bright sunshine, nodding to an officer to call off the search.

I squinted. It was the next day. "I can't believe I lasted all night out here alone."

"I lost a good twelve hours of my life because I didn't sleep a wink. What happened, Tink?"

I filled him in on everything that happened at the stables.

"No one had a clue where you were." He gave me a no-nonsense look, and I didn't complain because he was right. "That needs to change in the future." I nodded emphatically, and he kissed the top of my head. "You can thank Morty for bringing me a Dolce Vita Stables flyer. I drove in that direction, and nearly had a heart attack when I saw your car flipped over." He looked down at me and took a deep breath. "The scariest moment was kneeling down to look inside your totaled Bug. I was terrified of what I would see."

"I can only imagine. I'm so sorry."

"I know." He tightened his arms around me. "The relief I felt when you weren't inside was short lived after I saw your footprints heading into the woods. I tried to ping your cell phone, but it was dead." He gave me a pointed look, no words necessary. "We've been looking for you all night with Morty leading the way. Most of the town showed up. Let's just say you have a lot of fans."

"That was the scariest night of my life." A sob slipped out of my clogged throat.

"You shouldn't have been driving in such bad weather."

I shook my head hard. "I didn't lose control and go off the road, Mitch."

He frowned. "Then what happened?"

"Someone at the stables sliced my tire, but I didn't realize it until the spot I pulled over. I got out to check on it, and saw headlights coming straight at me. I ran out of the way just in time. The person smashed into my car on purpose, Mitch."

He cursed under his breath.

"I took off running, and they followed for a while, but I outran them. Someone tried to kill me, Mitch, and something tells me they're not through with me yet."

"Then, clearly, they don't know who your husband is. If anyone lays a finger on you, they're mine. Consequences be damned."

"I can't believe my Bug is totaled," I said that afternoon at the police station. My heart hurt. I loved that car so much. Dawson and Big Don both agreed she was beyond resuscitation. I needed time to grieve before I bought a new vehicle.

Mitch had insisted I see Doc Wilcox first, who confirmed my ankle was sprained. I had a walking boot on and was assured my ankle would be fine in a few weeks. Other than a few scrapes and bruises, Tina confirmed the baby and I were fine. After we left the doctor's office, we went home where I showered and my amazing husband made me a huge plate of cheese fries. I thanked him by grabbing some veggies as a side dish. Now we were at the station where I had just finished giving my statement.

"I'm just so glad you're okay," Mayor Cromwell said.

"I told everyone she shouldn't be allowed to consult on this case given her condition, and I was right," Mitch pointed out.

"My condition had nothing to do with someone slicing my tire and smashing into my car, Detective Grumpy Pants," I countered.

"It might have slowed down your running," Chief Spencer added, supporting my husband as usual.

Mitch crossed his arms and sat back, gloating. He was determined to get his way one way or another.

"Oh, please, we all know I'm no athlete," I said. "Just ask Wally. Or your wife. I'm pretty sure I took out her knee with my Zumba moves."

Chief Spencer nodded, wincing at Mitch.

"Okay, then what about your ability to think clearly?" Mitch was grasping at straws to get me kicked off helping the police with this case. "You're the one who keeps saying you have pregnancy brain, whatever that means."

"Look, children," Captain Walker said with an authoritative tone. "Sunny stays on the case," he stared Mitch down and I grinned, "but," he leveled a serious look at me, "you are not to take any more chances by going rogue on your own. You are to keep Detective Stone in the loop at all times. Am I clear?"

My shoulders wilted, and I nodded.

"Good. Now, what have you found?" he asked Mitch.

"Detective Fuller and I went back to the crash site. We were able to trace the tire tracks and paint left on Sunny's car to one person."

"Who?" I asked.

Mitch met my eyes. "Rich Hastings."

I gasped. "When I was at Dolce Vita Stables, I overheard him arguing with Mark Silverman." I had no choice but to tell what I knew about both of them since Rich had obviously tried to kill me. I only hoped Mark would understand. "They were involved in an illegal gambling ring with insider tips about the horses and jockeys that Mark supplied. Mark wanted out, but Rich was blackmailing him, threatening to go public and ruin his career as a respected equine vet. Apparently, there were other big players involved."

"Detective Stone, look into that," Captain Walker said, then asked me, "Anything else, Sunny?"

"Well, I waited until Rich left and I confronted Mark. He said he would stop, and I was giving him a chance to do the right thing. Maybe Rich overheard us. When I walked to my car, I had the strongest sensation that someone was watching me."

"He could have followed you and been desperate enough to try to shut you up before you could tell anyone," Captain Walker pointed out.

"You have a point, especially after his alibi for the night of Audra's murder didn't check out, either. He said he was with Mark, but Zoe said that wasn't true and Mark confirmed her statement. If Rich was desperate enough to try to kill me, then he just might have killed Audra. I'll look into that."

"*I'll* look into that," Mitch clarified, then relented, "You do what you do best."

I eyed him with suspicion. "And that is what?"

"You know." He waved his hand about as if it were a wand. "Your hocus pocus stuff." He looked uncomfortable with the conversation, but I was thrilled he had initiated it. Maybe there was hope he actually really did believe in my ability after all. "See if you can get a read on Rich Hastings, or anyone for that matter. Doesn't it help when you touch something that belongs to the person?"

"Yes, that does help." I looked at the captain. "If you can get a search warrant for the Divinity Hotel, I'll go through Audra's things and see if I can get a read on Rich." I looked at my husband. "And if you can bring me anything of Rich's, I might be able to pick up a reading from that as well."

"Deal, but Sunny," my husband looked at me with such worry filled eyes as he pleaded, "please don't go alone. I can't take another night like last night." Mitch rubbed his temples, the shadows beneath his eyes more pronounced.

"Okay," I said softly, my heart so full of love for this man.

"Okay?" His hands paused. "That easy? What's the catch?"

"There's no catch." I smiled and reached out to squeeze his hand. "I honestly can't take another night like last night either."

"Finally, we're all in agreement," Captain Walker said. "Now, let's go get this creep. Maybe we'll get lucky and wrap up the murder investigation while we're at it."

"One can only hope," Chief Spencer said, "because if none of these leads pan out, things aren't looking good for Sean O'Malley."

20

L   ater that day, Jo and I made a trip to the Divinity Hotel.

The Divinity Hotel was small but quaint and showcased the Art Deco style of the 1930s inspired by the artists of Paris. The streamlined, polished look only added to the hotel's appeal. Lacquered wood furniture combined with brushed steel and lined with exotic zebra skin upholstery were scattered about the lobby. Colorful starburst motifs in exotic greens and oranges with small amounts of black and gold arranged in geometric shapes covered the floors and walls. But what caught the eye the most was the fireplace.

It wasn't just a fireplace used for heat. It was the focal point of the lobby. The centerpiece. A combination of mahogany, walnut and oak wood was used to create the mantel because these woods were easy to carve and featured contrasting grains as part of the design. Carved beading, flowers and leaves lined the frieze, and a beveled mirror was built right into the center, surrounded by hand-painted tiles.

It really was a sight to behold.

Chuck Web was all too happy to talk to us. In the

past, he wanted nothing to do with us. Now that he was happily married to Abigail and a father to a baby girl, he was all about keeping Divinity safe. He led us to Audra's room and unlocked the door to let us in.

"The night of Ms. Grimshaw's murder, Greg Gates asked me if she'd come back from the Psychic Fair yet. I told him I hadn't seen her. Then he told me the door to her room was open. He said nothing was taken that he could tell, so I didn't think much of it. It was a mess. I just thought Audra was a slob or something. Now I'm wondering if someone broke in and was looking for something, or if Greg himself ransacked the place. They weren't on the best of terms at the time, and she'd made him get his own room." Chuck looked around the room warily. "I wish this case would hurry up and close. I don't like murder being associated with my place of business."

"You and me both, Mr. Webb," I said. Too much time had passed, and I was worried our leads were running cold. "How's Abby and the baby?"

His whole face lit up. "They're doing great. Just wait until your little one arrives. They grow so fast. I wish time would slow down."

"I hear that," Jo said. "My boys grow bigger every day, I swear."

"That's what happens when you have Sasquatch cubs." I laughed.

"You should talk." She grunted. "You're married to a Grizzly, which isn't much smaller."

"Don't remind me." My stomach flipped, and I put my hand over it and whispered, "You'd better be a petite girl like your mama."

Jo snorted, obviously having heard me. "Good luck with that."

"Thank you, Mr. Webb," I said, ignoring Jo's comment and refusing to dwell on bears of any kind. "We'll take it from here."

"I'll be right up front if you need anything else."

"Greg Gates told me he'd read about Michael Mc-Masters, the affair, and the baby from Audra's diary." I looked at Jo. "I'm sure he found that in her room, but why tell Chuck the door was unlocked?"

"I'm sure he didn't want Chuck to think he broke the lock, and he probably was looking for Audra." Jo walked through the door. "I think someone *was* in the room before him. You said Rich Hastings was blackmailing Mark Silverman. So maybe he ransacked Audra's place, looking for something to blackmail her with. That seems to be his thing. Obviously, he never found the diary since Greg has it. I wonder if he found anything else?"

"Only one way to find out."

"Don't we need gloves or something?"

"The police have already gathered all their evidence. I'm looking for something they can't see themselves." I walked around the room, touching various items, waiting for the hum of energy to fill me.

"Are you getting anything?"

"Not yet."

"Wait, what's this?" Jo pointed to a seam in the mattress that had been hand stitched. "I'm pretty sure that's not how this mattress was made."

"How did you even spot that?"

"I'm one of eight kids. We always had secret hiding spots if we wanted to keep anything to ourselves. My older sister had one just like this on her mattress." Jo grabbed scissors and cut the thread, tugging the string free. Pulling the material of the mattress apart, the corner of something was visible.

"Wait." I pulled out a pair of rubber gloves and

handed them to her. "I guess we do need to use these. The police definitely didn't see that."

I put on a pair of gloves myself and opened a Ziplock bag. Jo pulled the item all the way out and handed it to me. "It's a notebook."

I opened the cover and saw a list of all the people in Divinity that Audra had read, with notes beneath each one on what she had seen. Personal, intimate details about their past and their future. "This is a lot of information that I'm pretty sure many of these people don't want the public to know about." I looked at Jo. "And Rich Hasting's name is right at the top." I closed the notebook and slid it into the clean Ziplock bag. then put it in my tote bag to bring back to the police station.

"I wonder if he knew about this?" Jo asked. "I bet Audra threatened him with it so he would back off after he shouted at her in front of everyone. This is probably what he was looking for."

"Him or any number of the people on that list. It's clear Audra used her gift for evil to get whatever she wanted." I sighed. "That's such a shame. This is the kind of behavior that gives genuine psychics a bad rap."

"Well, let's go. It's getting late and I think we've probably found all we're going to." Jo headed for the door.

I started to follow her, then I saw a shiny object on the floor under the bed. "Wait." I bent down and picked up the item. It looked like an earring.

My eyes narrowed into tunnel vision, with everything else in the room fading away like it always did when I had a vision. I was in a woman's body. She walked quickly down the hall of this very hotel and came upon Audra's open door. Someone had already been here. Glancing left then right, I slipped inside. It had to be here. This was the only place I'd worn them. I reached up and felt my empty earlobe.

I searched around the room, looking everywhere possible, but I couldn't find it. My heart pounded and I began to sweat. Audra couldn't know I was here now or that I'd been here before. Neither of them could know that I saw them, and that I knew the secret Audra was hiding. I needed proof, especially after what had happened when I gave birth. I was hiding in the closet, and I saw them together. I felt anger and frustration but not love. No matter what the cost, I had to find a way to keep this quiet. We had a deal. I refused to let this ruin everything I'd worked so hard to build.

My head jerked up. Someone was coming. I had to leave without it. I couldn't risk getting caught. I slipped out the door and scurried down the hall in the other direction just in time.

"Sunny," Jo repeated, pulling me out of my vision. "Are you okay?"

I blinked several times. "I'm fine, I just had a vision." I looked down at the earring I held in my hand.

"Did you see someone in this room?"

"Yes," I nodded. "But it wasn't Rich Hastings."

JO DROPPED ME OFF AT THE INN, AND I BORROWED Granny Gert's car. I hated being without a vehicle, but Jo had to get back to work. I drove the evidence I'd collected to the police station, and everyone on the sidewalks steered clear of the street as I approached until they realized I was the driver and not Granny Gert. Let's just say her big ol' caddy gave people the vapors, considering she ran stop signs and jumped curbs on a regular basis.

The woman should not have a driver's license. After she'd failed her road test five times because of nerves, I'd taught her how to drive, but even I knew she wasn't a good driver. An unfortunate mix-up in some special herbal brownies relaxed her just enough that she passed with flying colors.

Now she drove everywhere, much to the entire town's dismay.

I rolled the windows down and kept waving my arm out the window to keep from giving anyone a heart attack. It was exhausting. After I turned the evidence in, I decided to leave the car there and walk down Main Street to meet Mitch for dinner at Nikko's restaurant. I was almost there when I spotted Danny McMasters coming out of the Town Hall and walking alone at a quick pace.

I hobbled along with my sprained ankle, keeping watch on which direction he went. He traveled quite a bit down the street, away from his father's office and the library where his mother held her auxiliary meetings. He looked over his shoulder, and I ducked behind some people and pretended to study the window display of a small boutique.

He turned back around and kept going, so I resumed following him.

My phone dinged, so I glanced at it.

Mitch: Where are you?

Me: On Main Street.

Mitch: I have a table for us.

Me: Be there soon.

Mitch: I thought you had your grandmother's car

Me: Left it at the station. Walking. Safer.

Mitch: I repeat, where are you?

Me: Dumpster Diving. Gotta go.

Danny had turned down an alley between two buildings while I was on the phone to Mitch. I peeked around the corner. I saw him throw something in a dumpster, then slip around the back out of sight.

I waited a few minutes to be sure he was gone, then I crept toward the dumpster. This brought back memories of another time I'd had to dive in a dumpster. I was not a fan of trash, but I needed to know what was so secret that Danny felt the need to go to the far end of Main Street to throw the item away when there was a dumpster right by Town Hall he could have used.

The dumpster was pretty full. Trash day was tomorrow. There was no way I could go into Nikko's Italian restaurant smelling of garbage. I groaned, already lamenting the big plate of spaghetti and meatballs I would miss. I climbed the best that I could with a bum ankle. At least I had a sneaker on the other foot, but my daisy sundress would never be the same. I carefully pulled myself over the edge and landed on a pile of soft, smelly trash bags.

Whatever Danny had thrown in here had to be small, because he was able to toss it one handed into the dumpster. I'd been too far away to see what it was. I just knew it wasn't in a trash bag. So, I started moving trash bags around, looking for loose items. I was amazed at all the crazy items people threw in dumpsters. Construction materials, furniture, a mailbox, gross half-eaten fast-food bags.

Something scurried across my foot, and I squealed.

"Are you about done?" came a deep voice from above me.

I looked up at Detective Grumpy Pants, not even surprised to see him anymore. "Almost?"

"I take it we're not eating out."

"Not after this." I gagged.

"Why are you in a dumpster?" he asked in an almost this is normal behavior of my pregnant wife acceptance tone. "Or don't I want to know?"

"Oh, you'll want to know this," I said excitedly.

"I'm all ears, Tink."

"I was on my way to Nikko's, which I'm totally bummed about not getting to order spaghetti, or wait, maybe the chicken parme—"

"Sunny, focus."

"Sorry. Anyway, I was on my way to meet you when I spotted Danny McMasters coming out of Town Hall."

"His father is the head of the Town Council and has an office in there. His son leaving that building is not unusual."

"True, but there was something about the fast way he was walking and looking around suspiciously. So, I listened to my gut and followed him."

"And?"

"And he ducked down this alley and threw something in this dumpster."

Mitch pointed his finger a me. "If this turns out to be his leftover burger or something, you're in big trouble, Tink."

"It won't be, Grumpy Pants. I just know it. Call it a hunch."

He sighed and swung his leg over the edge.

"What are you doing?"

"My mama always said, if you can't beat 'em, join 'em."

"Wait, you're seriously going to join me in dumpster diving?"

"If it will help get us home quicker, then yes. I'm starving."

"You won't be by the time we're done. It's disgusting in here."

"I see that." He threw a soggy piece of lettuce out of the way. "You owe me big time for this, Tink."

An hour later after we had searched every nook and cranny of the dumpster, Mitch had turned into a hangry Grump Butt and was at the end of his rope. "That's it," he said. "We're done."

"Yes, we are." I held up an item triumphantly.

He narrowed his eyes, inspecting the item, and then his eyes widened. "Is that what I think it is?"

"It sure looks like it. I think, Detective Stone, that we just found our burner phone."

21

T he next morning, I was coming out of Doc Wilcox's office after he rechecked my ankle when I saw Willow Goodbody enter Rita Haynes office. Last I knew, Rita didn't believe in or much less like psychics, so what on earth was Willow doing there? Rita's office wasn't even open yet.

I waited until Willow left, then I crept into the building and made my way down the hall to see Rita. I knocked on her door, and she opened it, startled to see me. "Sorry, I'm closed." She started to shut her door.

"I saw Willow Goodbody come out only moments ago."

Rita hesitated, then looked around before stepping back and letting me in. "It's not what you think."

I just sat there, waiting.

"Okay, so maybe it is," she finally said and took a seat across from me. "I've sworn in front of everyone that I don't believe in psychics. My patients know this. My reputation will be ruined if people know I went to see a psychic myself."

"I don't understand."

"Ever since my mother died unexpectedly, I've been having a hard time dealing with the loss. We were very close. She was a therapist as well. I followed in her footsteps, and all of my beliefs I got from her."

"I'm very sorry for your loss."

"Thank you. Anyway, I tried therapy, and I even tried to fix myself. Nothing worked. I started growing short with my patients and pushing them away. When they turned to Audra, I lashed out at them and blamed her. It wasn't until I met Willow unexpectedly, the night of Audra's murder. I had just had an argument with Audra before the storm hit. Then when I started to leave like everyone else, I ran into Willow in her tent."

"But she's a psychic too."

"I know. I didn't want anything to do with her, but she's not like Audra. She saw my mother beside me and started telling me all these things my mother wanted me to know. She knew things about my mother that I had never told anyone. I ended up staying there until almost one in the morning. I left that tent a changed person."

"I'm glad you can see that not all of us are evil. Many of us try to help others just like you do."

"I'm a believer now for sure. Willow has helped me so much. I just don't know how to tell my patients and not have them think I'm a liar now as well."

"Just be honest with them. People change and grow, including you. They might benefit to know that you're not perfect either."

"Maybe you're right."

"The Lowenthal Twins told me you pushed them away. I think they could use your help now more than ever after what Danny McMasters did to them."

"You're right. I'll reach out to them tomorrow. I'm sorry for how nasty I was. The stages of grief can turn us into people we don't even recognize."

"I understand. And just so you know, you actually helped me a lot. My mother and I have a much better relationship because of your advice."

She smiled at me, and I glimpsed the therapist I first saw before she found out who I was. "I'm glad. I really do hope you find the killer. As for Willow, I can vouch that she was with me and not Greg Gates. She honestly just finds the man attractive, and I'm pretty sure he loves himself more than he ever loved Audra or any other woman."

"Good to know. Thank you, Ms. Haynes. For everything."

"Thank you." She reached out and grabbed my hand. "And just know you can come see me anytime you need to talk. I mean that."

"The same goes for you." Which might be sooner than I thought because two more suspects had just been cleared, and Sean was looking guiltier than ever.

MITCH AND I SAT IN THE INTERROGATION ROOM AT Divinity Police Department. Michael and Beth Mc-Masters sat across from us with their son Danny between them.

"I don't understand what this is all about," Michael said.

"Why do you need to see all of us?" Beth asked.

"Because this matter involves your son, Danny," Mitch said, looking at them both with his most intimidating detective expression.

Michael and Beth both looked at their son in surprise.

"I didn't do anything illegal. Those girls deserved

to have the world see that they were lying to everyone."

"What are you talking about, honey?" Beth asked, rubbing his back.

"The videos. Ginger and Honey are fakes. They spent all their college money to make stupid videos because Audra told them to. I can't help if they suck. They should have thought of that before they were mean to me."

"Audra didn't tell them to do that," I clarified. "They simply interpreted her advice in the wrong way."

"Whatever," Danny said. "It doesn't matter anyway. They're still liars. They pretend to be cool, but they're really losers. And they called me a loser? At least I'm real, so I showed the world the real them."

Michael sucked in a breath of air. "You're the one behind the Lowenthal Twins' leaked videos?" he asked Danny, looking disappointed. He played golf with their father. "That wasn't very nice."

"Dude, you don't have a right to lecture me. They weren't nice to me at all, and you certainly haven't been nice to Mom."

"Danny, don't," Beth said, glancing at Michael who had turned red faced. "This isn't the time or place."

"I've had it," Michael finally spat. "I am sick of everyone thinking I am the only person who has done something wrong. Your perfect mother has been having an affair for years with Cal Stanton. The only reason no one knows is because he didn't die."

Beth gasped. "You got Audra pregnant, Michael. The rule was supposed to be no scandals or shame upon our family name."

"Rule?" Danny looked ill.

"Scandals?" Michael glared at Beth. "You should

talk. You let me believe Danny was my son. I'd say you've been hiding the biggest scandal of all. He looks just like Cal. Did you really think I would never find out?"

"I don't care if you found out. You're the reason I lost his twin sister. I will never forgive you for making my life so stressful I delivered too early."

"Delivered another man's children, darling. Don't forget that."

"Because of you, I can't have any more children yet you got a woman half your age pregnant."

Danny gaped at his mother and then his father. "What is wrong with you people?" He shoved his chair back. "I don't want to be around either of you. I'm out of here."

"Sit down, Danny," Mitch said in his best firm, no-nonsense detective tone. "You're not going anywhere."

Mitch pulled a bagged item from inside his jacket and set it on the table in front of everyone. Danny's eyes grew huge as he sat back down slowly.

"Do you recognize this?"

Danny started to shake his head no, but I added, "I followed you out of your father's office down Main Street to the dumpster at the end. There's no use denying it, Danny. Your prints are all over it."

"What is that?" Beth asked warily.

"The burner phone we've been looking for," Mitch answered.

"The one used to harass Audra with?" Michael asked, sounding defeated.

"The very one," Mitch responded.

"Why?" Beth asked Danny with a shaky voice.

"Because I thought Dad was the bad guy. He wasn't very careful at hiding his affairs. I was trying to protect you, Mom, but you're just as bad. You're both sick."

She tried to touch him, but he jerked away. "I hated Audra for what she was doing to our family. I thought by harassing her, she would go away, but I didn't kill her." He looked at Mitch and me with frightened eyes. "I went home. I promise. Our housekeeper can verify that. Ask the twins where they were. They hated Audra too, and they said they were with that stupid bodybuilder. He denied that, and they still haven't admitted where they were."

"Why were you coming out of your dad's office?" I asked.

"I planted the phone there to frame him, then I changed my mind and threw it in the dumpster instead. I didn't want to ruin our family either, but who cares now. It's already ruined. I want to divorce both my parents and go live with my grandmother."

"One thing at a time. You're an adult, Danny," Mitch said, letting his words sink in. "Let's worry about the crime of harassment and clearing your name of murder first."

"WHAT A CRAZY FEW DAYS," I SAID TO JO AS I JOINED her on her lunch break at Smokey Jo's.

Zoe sat down with us. "I know. So much has happened, but yet I'm more worried more than ever. Who's left as suspects?"

"Well, Rita Haynes and Willow Goodbody have both been cleared since they were together the night of the murder. Beth McMasters was with Cal Stanton while Michael and Danny were both at home according to their housekeeper, unless she's lying to keep her job. Danny obviously lied about his father being home because he hates him and was trying to get him in trouble. Mark Silverman was talking to you, so he's good." Zoe nodded, and I continued, "I'm pretty sure Rich Hastings was going through Audra's room at the time she was being murdered, most likely looking for something to blackmail her with."

"Tell her what we found at the hotel," Jo said.

"I found an earring and had a vision. I think Beth McMasters went through the room after Rich, looking for her earring. I think she was there looking for proof that Audra was pregnant with her husband's child or for a way to ruin her. She admitted protecting her family's name and reputation was the most important thing to her."

"Wow, that's crazy the lengths people will go to for their reputations." Zoe shook her head.

"The door was already open," I continued, "then Beth left when I'm assuming Greg showed up and found Audra's diary. Greg still doesn't have a solid alibi and neither does Rich, but he's in jail for trying to kill me. Not to mention, we have some new names in Audra's notebook who might have murdered her to keep their secrets safe. Don't worry, Zoe, there's still hope for Sean."

"If you say so," Zoe said. "It's all so confusing to me."

"I know, but you have to keep the faith." I squeezed her hand.

"Yeah, you never know what can happen when you least expect it." Jo refilled our drinks and opened a new bag of chips. "I remember feeling this exact same way when Cole was accused of murder. It's a horrible feeling and hard to stay positive."

"It sure is. I just wish something more solid would happen." Zoe pushed her food away as if she had no appetite. "It's so hard to keep Sean in a good headspace. The last thing we need is for more people to be cleared as suspects."

"Wow," Jo stared across the room, her mouth falling open before adding, "they look like completely different people."

"Who?" I asked, following her gaze.

"Ginger and Honey Lowenthal," she clarified, pointing across the room.

"Oh, I forgot about them. They don't have an alibi yet either." I stood. "This might be the break we need, Zoe. If you'll excuse me, ladies, I have some questions to ask."

I walked over to the girls' table and was shocked. Different wasn't a strong enough word. The extensions were out of their hair, which was half as thick and less jet black and pin straight, falling only to their shoulders in dark brown waves. Their fake eyelashes were off, and their faces not caked in makeup anymore. A few freckles and pimples graced their cheeks, but at least they looked natural and real.

"Ladies, I must say, I like the new look," I said as I sat down.

"You do?" Ginger asked. "I feel naked."

"You don't need all that fake stuff. People will relate to you more when you're being your true authentic selves."

"That's what Ms. Haynes said," Honey replied.

I was happy Rita had reached out to them.

"We didn't have a choice," Ginger added. "The real reason we didn't tell you where we were the night of Audra's murder is because we didn't want anyone to know we looked like this. Just like we paid Danny to help us with our videos, we paid Mindy Marshall to help us with our look."

"Who's that?"

"A makeup artist and hair wizard we met in college. She created the look after hours, but when we ran out of money, she dumped us. That's who we were with during the time Audra was murdered."

I wrote down the name. "Thank you for being honest. I'll will get in touch with Mindy and get back to you. So, what are your plans now?"

"To go back to college. We'll have loans now, but that's a small price to pay after all that we did," Ginger admitted.

"Yeah, we've learned a lot from this," Honey added.

"I'm glad to hear it," I said, but secretly my heart sank over yet again two more suspects being cleared.

"**M**r. Ventura, please come in," I said. I'd gone back home after lunch to see to a few clients and had just finished giving a reading to the mayor. "What can I do for you?"

He shoved his hands in his jean pockets, his shirt was wrinkled and salt and pepper hair a mess. "My wife would have a fit if she knew I was here. She hates our dirty laundry being aired, but I don't know what more to do. Sweet Life lost again." He started pacing across my foyer floor.

"I'm so sorry. Maybe he's trying to tell you he needs a rest."

Antonio stopped pacing and stared at me, looking a little crazy.

"Mr. Ventura, are you okay?"

He shook off his crazed look. "Please, call me Antonio. I'm sorry for acting so strangely. I'm desperate if I'm being honest. I don't have another horse ready for the races. Unfortunately, I made some poor investment choices in the past that have caught up with me. People...bad people...want their money. Even my wife didn't know how bad things were. I've let everyone down." He shook his head. "With Sweet Life continuing to lose, I don't have the money to get out of debt. I went to see Audra Grimshaw, and she saw this coming. Now that she's gone, I don't have anyone to turn to." He looked me in the eye, pleading with me. "Can you help me, Mrs. Stone?"

I had seen his name in Audra's book, implementing him in the same illegal gambling ring as Mark Silverman and Rich Hastings, but I wouldn't tell him I knew that. "Actually, my next appointment canceled this afternoon, so you're in luck. Follow me to my Sanctuary, and I'll see if I can help you."

He followed me into my sanctuary, and I instructed him to take his shoes off and sit cross-legged on the yoga mat. After he complied, I sat across from him cross-legged and then took his hands in mine.

"I want you to close your eyes and relax your body. Clear your mind of everything except what question you wish to have answered. Now breathe slowly and steadily while concentrating on your question."

He did as I instructed. I closed my eyes as well and took a few slow deep breaths myself. Concentrating on his energy, I let my mind focus solely on him. My vision transformed into tunnel vision once more like it always did when I picked up a reading. I was standing in the same stable that Mark and Rich had been arguing in, except they weren't there and the time wasn't the present.

It had to be around seventy-five years ago. Not much had changed over the years. The family had always taken great pride in keeping the stables in mint condition. I was looking through the eyes of a man around thirty years old. He felt familiar somehow, but I couldn't imagine how. Pulling out his magnifying glass, he bent down and inspected the inside of the stall. He methodically searched every aspect of that stall and stopped when he spotted something. Pulling out a handkerchief, he picked up the item, careful not to touch it with his fingers and then he stood up.

The door to the stable flew open.

"Detective Fellini, you're trespassing," the man boomed.

"Salvatore Ventura, just the man I wanted to see," Detective Fellini responded.

"You could have found me in my office. What are you doing in my barn?"

"Looking for this." Fellini held the item out.

"A needle doesn't prove anything," Salvatore responded. "Horses get medication all the time, especially race horses. It's hard to keep them in prime racing condition."

"Ah, but I bet the drops in the syringe will show you weren't medicating your horse. You were doping him with steroids to better his chances of winning. That's cheating the system, not to mention dangerous for the horse, and illegal." Detective Fellini wrapped the syringe more securely in his handkerchief and tucked it into his jacket. "Mr. Ventura, I'm going to have to take you in."

"I'm not going anywhere," he pulled out a gun, "but you are."

I felt the shock and fear sweep through my body, my pulse picking up speed at an alarming rate. My mind whirled with different scenarios for a way out. Detective Fellini reached for his own weapon, but he wasn't quick enough. Salvatore Ventura shot him in the gut. My insides felt the burn of the bullet sear through my stomach. I cried out, finding it hard to breathe. Salvatore pointed the gun at my head this time, but voices sounded outside the barn. He hesitated, then tucked his gun away and slipped outside to steer the workers away, saying something about having to put a horse down.

I knew I only had moments before he returned to finish the job. It wouldn't matter anyway because the bullet to my gut was fatal. I knew that. My heart pained for all I would miss. For my dear love. I vowed right then and there not to rest until justice was served. A noise in the barn sounded, and the answer stood before me. I reached out a hand—

"What is it? What do you see?" Antonio asked frantically.

I started out of my vision and opened my eyes, then recanted what I saw.

"No, no, no," Antonio cried out, "this can't be true."

"Mr. Ventura, that was in the past. You don't have to pay for your ancestor's crimes."

He just kept shaking his head. "You don't understand." He surged to his feet and shoved them into his shoes. "I have to go."

"But, Antonio, I can help you. Let me finish your reading and—"

"No!" he shouted; his eyes more crazed than ever. "This can't be happening again," he blurted as he ran out of my house.

Mitch came running in with Morty right beside him. "Sunny? What happened? Are you okay?"

"I'm fine." Morty jumped into my lap and stared deeply into my eyes. "Really, buddy, I'm okay."

My detective husband inspected every inch of me before finally asking, "What was that all about?"

"Honestly, I'm not quite sure. But one thing is certain. Antonio Ventura is not a well man."

Mitch frowned.

Morty hissed.

And I had a premonition that justice was about to be served.

THAT EVENING WE WENT TO MY PARENTS' INN FOR dinner.

"Boys oh day, it's a beautiful evening out," Great-Grandma Tootsie said. "A great night to barbecue." She handed Harry a tray of ribs and chicken slathered in a mouth-watering sauce by the smell of it. "Fiona and Granny Gert are getting the pasta and potato salads ready. Let me know when the meat is almost ready, and I will make the tossed salad."

"Come on, Donald, I could use some help," Harry said, and my father gladly followed. "Mitch, I imagine you do most of the cooking at your house." My father winked at me, and I smirked. "Want to lend us a hand, son?"

"Sure thing." Mitch grabbed a cooler of beer and followed them out, looking over his shoulder at me pleadingly.

"Come on, Mom, let's join them. Summer is so short; we really should take advantage of the Vitamin D and warm weather."

"Why not?" She grabbed a pitcher of lemonade. "Be a doll and bring the glasses, darling."

"Of course." I followed my mother outside and we sat on the patio while the men pretended to be grill masters.

"How's your ankle?" my mother asked with genuine concern, and a warmth filled my heart.

"It's much better. I went to physical therapy, and that really helped." I sipped my lemonade, my stomach grumbling over the delicious aromas coming from the grill. "How is your strength training class with Wally going?"

"Wally is amazing, but I'm sure you already know that. There isn't a thing that man can't do. And Olivia Ventura has been a big help in me learning the proper form. We both feel much safer at protecting ourselves with a killer still on the loose out there. You should definitely have Mitch give you some self-defense pointers."

"That's a good idea. I'll be sure to do that."

"I only wish Olivia and Tony could have joined us. I guess he didn't feel well. She wasn't sure what was wrong with him."

I wondered if it had anything to do with the reading I had given him. He didn't want her to know, so I didn't mention it. "That's too bad. I hope he feels better soon."

"Me too. I don't think anyone feels that great with everything that's been going on in Divinity lately."

"Hopefully, the investigation will be over with soon."

Toots, Granny Gert and Fiona came out carrying all the salads. The table was already set with outdoor picnic style tablecloth and dishes. Mitch ended up doing most of the grilling because the other two couldn't see if the meat was done with their eyesight. They carried the trays of cooked meats to the table as Mitch took them off the grill.

"This was a great idea, Toots. Everything looks and smells amazing." I picked up my fork, about to dig in, when Mitch's phone rang.

"Detective Stone here." He listened to the caller, and his face grew serious. "Got it." He wrote something down in his notebook. "I'm on my way." He hung up.

We all stared at him in anticipation.

"Well, what happened? Something's obviously wrong by the look on your face," I said, my stomach twisting into knots and my appetite suddenly gone from the strange feeling in my gut.

"Antonio Ventura just killed himself."

MITCH AND I WENT TO DOLCE VITA STABLES TOGETHER. The crime scene investigators were combing over Antonio's office where he lay slumped over his desk after shooting himself. The ambulance was waiting to take the body to the coroner's office.

Olivia Ventura sat in the living room, dabbing her red swollen eyes, still softly crying. "I don't understand why my Tony would do such a thing? Our daughters are away at college, thank goodness. I don't know how I'm supposed to tell them their father is dead. Worse, that he took his own life." I handed her more tissues, and she blew her nose.

"Did you know about your husband's illegal gambling addiction?" I hated to ask, but we still had questions that needed answers.

She shook her head. "I knew he was stressed out over Sweet Life not winning. I had no idea our financial situation was that bad. He never wanted to bother me with worrisome details, so he took care of everything and let me and the girls do whatever we wanted." She cried harder. "How am I supposed to show my face in society now? People will have pity on me and think we're poor. I will *not* be pitied. I am a Ventura." She sat up straighter, reminding me so much of my mother. "I'm so angry at him for putting us in this position."

"Mrs. Ventura—"

"Call me Olivia, dear."

I reached out and patted her arm. "Olivia, did Tony tell you I gave him a reading earlier today?"

Her eyes grew wide as she stared at me. "Why, no, he didn't. Do you think that's why he killed himself? What on earth did you see?"

"I saw his ancestor murder a detective years ago over horse doping."

She looked scandalized as she gasped. "A Ventura would never do something like that. We have an impeccable reputation to uphold. Maybe you were mistaken in your vision. Even you said sometimes it takes a while for you to figure out what your vision might mean. There has to be another explanation for what you saw."

"My vision was crystal clear. There was no mistaking Salvatore Ventura pointing a gun at Detective Fellini and shooting him in the stomach after Fellini found a steroid syringe in the horse stall in the barn."

"That doesn't mean Antonio's ancestor was the one doping the horses. It could have been someone else. Maybe even Fellini himself."

"It wasn't. I heard their conversation."

"I'm sorry if I can't go off a reading as proof. I'm not saying I don't believe in your ability, Sunny, but gambling and having financial troubles are bad enough. I can't have what's left of my stables' reputation ruined by a psychic vision which may or may not be true." She dabbed the corners of her eyes with a handkerchief. "Surely, you understand how upsetting that would be for my family."

"I get it, but I know what I saw, Mrs. Ventura. You must have come across some family history on Salvatore Ventura."

"Nothing that scandalous, I can assure you."

"Well, your husband had a crazed look in his eyes when he heard the story, and he kept saying how I didn't understand and this couldn't be happening again. Do you know what he meant by that?"

"Not at all. My husband was under a great deal of pressure to keep Dolce Vita Stables on top. He didn't have as much luck as his predecessors. I think that pressure made him snap. He never should have made those bad investments." She shook her head. "I just never expected him to take his own life." She started crying again. "Nothing will ever be the same again."

"I'm so sorry." I took her hand in mine.

"I don't know if Antonio told you, but Audra Grimshaw gave him a reading during the Psychic Fair. According to a notebook she kept, she saw the illegal gambling ring he was involved with. I think he might have killed her to keep the news from getting out, not knowing about the notebook. I'm sure the guilt over that and the stress of running a losing stable drove him over the edge. Once I gave him this latest reading and saw everything, he feared the truth was about come out so he killed himself before others in the gambling ring came for him or you and your girls."

I released a soft sigh over my logical deduction, worthy of Grumpy Pants approval. But still, something didn't feel right. Did I miss something somewhere?

Mitch joined us with a grave look on his face. "The crew found a suicide note that must have fallen under his desk.

Olivia sucked in a sharp breath and covered her mouth with both hands. "C-Can I see it? What does it say?"

"It's already been taken in as evidence, but I took a

picture of it for you." Mitch brought up the picture on his phone and handed it to Olivia.

"I can't believe I was married to a murderer," Olivia whispered, looking stunned, shaking her head over and over in as if to banish the truth. "The girls are going to be devastated enough over his suicide, but the fact he is a murderer, as well, is going to shatter them." She placed her delicate hands over her face, her shoulders softly shaking.

"Again, I'm so sorry," I said. "If there is anything we can do, please don't hesitate to ask."

"Thank you, dear." She looked up at me with red-rimmed eyes. "You're lucky to be part of such a wonderful family."

We left, and I realized she was right. I was very lucky, and this was a reminder never to take my life for granted.

Because you never knew when it was going to be cut short.

23

A couple days later, we attended the funeral of Antonio Ventura. His daughters were there, standing on both sides of their mother, Olivia, who looked frail for the first time ever. The citizens of Divinity turned out in droves. It had been raining, but the sun came out now and a beautiful rainbow arched across the cemetery. People had liked Antonio and Olivia both. They were more saddened than anything over the turn of events.

Antonio's suicide note had said he couldn't live with the guilt and felt his family would be better off without him. After Audra Grimshaw did his reading and saw the gambling ring he was involved in, she was going to go to the police. He had to stop her from talking somehow. They'd argued and he'd strangled her, then pushed her into the electrified puddle to cover it up. He hadn't meant to kill her. No one deserved to die, but Audra Grimshaw had done a lot of people wrong.

Sean's name was cleared, and the case was closed.

I was happy about that so he and Zoe could get on with their future, but I did feel really bad for the Ventura family. I spotted Mark Silverman standing alone, staring at the casket after the service, looking genuinely upset. He'd lost his practice after what he had done and was awaiting trial of his own for the crimes he had committed. I approached him, feeling bad for the consequences of his poor choices.

"Hey, Mark. How are you?"

He shrugged, shoving his hands in his pockets. "I'm okay. What a mess this has all turned out to be. If I could do things differently, I would. Antonio was like a father to me. He didn't deserve this."

"I'm sorry for your loss. This is hard on everyone. Gambling is an addiction, and people can get a little crazy when money is involved."

"Yeah, especially when you mess with the wrong people." Mark looked like he wanted to say something more, then just said, "It's wrong and sad that he's gone this young. Things didn't have to be this way. This never should have happened."

"I know you don't like Sean much, but I also know you care a lot about Zoe still. You should know she's relieved and happy. They can finally start their life together."

He smiled a little sadly. "I'm glad. She deserves the best, and that's definitely not me." He walked away, his head hanging lower with every step.

I frowned. The poor guy was not himself for sure. I shrugged. There was nothing I could do about that, so I walked back to join my family, happy this investigation was finally over with. I was more than ready to focus on life rather than death for a change, like the new life growing inside of me. I smiled tenderly and put a hand over my tummy.

"I have food for Olivia and her girls. Would you help me bring it to their house?" my mother asked me.

"Sure, thing. What a nice idea." I turned to Mitch. "I'll see you back at the house later, okay?"

He nodded and kissed my cheek. "Be careful. The roads are still wet."

"Don't worry, I will."

"I can drop Donald off at the inn if you want," Mitch said to my mother.

"Thank you, Mitch." My mother hugged him. "You're a doll. I don't know what any of us would do without you."

"Let's hope you never have to find out." He winked.

I drove my mother's Prius because I still didn't have a car of my own. "The smells delicious," I said.

"The poor woman is a mess. They can't even afford their staff anymore." My mother tsked. "Great-Grandma Tootsie's lasagna will fix them right up, or at least as fixed up as they can be for the time being. There's salad and bread as well. Of course, Toots made enough to have leftovers for a week."

"I'm sure they'll appreciate it." After several minutes of silence, we finally reached Dolce Vita Stables. I pulled into the driveway by the main house and parked the car. We went inside and carried the food in.

"You ladies are a couple of angels," Olivia said, directing us to the kitchen where other trays of food lined the counter top. "I told everyone else I didn't want company, but I'm glad you two are here."

We set our goods down and followed Olivia and her daughters into the living room. "Are you sure?" I asked. "We don't have to stay."

"Sunny's right," my mother added. "We don't want to impose."

"Nonsense." Olivia smiled. "You have become my closest friend, Vivian. I find comfort with you around."

The women started talking about anything and everything. I glanced outside and did a double take. I waited a moment, but nothing more happened. I could have sworn I saw Morty. Every stable had barn cats, but this one was big and glowingly white. I excused myself and left them to talk while I went outside.

Another flash of white moved at lightning speed toward the horse stables. I'd know my cat anywhere. That was definitely Morty. I followed him inside, but then didn't see him anywhere. I walked into the building further, and stopped short. I blinked, unable to believe who I saw instead.

"What are you doing here?" I asked.

Mark jerked, his arm flinging the syringe he had been holding next to Sweet Life several feet away. He stared at me as if he didn't know what to say.

"Please tell me that's not what I think it is," I said.

"You don't understand. I have no choice, Sunny."

"Sure, you do," I responded. "Antonio is dead. You don't have to drug his horses for him anymore."

We both stared at the syringe and bolted at the same time.

I got there first.

As soon as I touched the syringe, I was sucked into the vision of Audra's death. I felt rage and hatred from the body I occupied. I shouted at Audra, but she laughed at me. She didn't take me seriously. I would show her. We fought, and then I wrapped my arms around her throat and squeezed. She looked at me with surprise as she realized just how serious I was. I hadn't meant to kill her. I just wanted to scare her into silence. I couldn't let her ruin everything I'd worked so hard to build. Once I realized what I'd done, I shoved her hard. She fell back into the electrified puddle, and her body fried.

I gasped, then gagged as I dropped the syringe. Stumbling back a step, I refocused on the present.

"I know who killed Audra Grimshaw," I said to Mark.

"Sunny, let me explain—"

"There's no need for that, Mark," a voice from behind me said.

I turned around slowly to see Olivia Ventura pointing a gun at me, and everything became crystal clear. "Oh, my gosh. You were the one drugging Sweet Life to win races, weren't you?"

"My husband didn't leave me any choice." Her face hardened. "He made some bad investments and put us in financial ruin. He never did have a good head for business. I had to be the strong one and do something."

"Why did you stop?" I was stalling, trying to think of a way out of my predicament, my gaze scanning the barn for something. Anything.

"I didn't stop by my choice. Your husband arrested Chance LeRoy for trying to sabotage your wedding. He had no idea Chance was my drug supplier."

"I don't understand how Mark is involved in any of this?"

Mark kept his eyes on the gun as he spoke, "Olivia knew of my illegal gambling ring with Rich and threatened to expose me and ruin my career if I didn't help her administer the drugs." His jaw hardened. "Antonio kept pushing me for answers on what was wrong with Sweet Life, but I couldn't tell him."

"Why didn't you just walk away from Olivia after the gambling ring was exposed?" I asked Mark, not understanding the point of continuing. His career had already been ruined at that point.

"Because doping horses to win races is a bigger offense. I couldn't risk that charge being added to my upcoming court case. Olivia kept pressing me to find her a new supplier when Sweet Life kept losing races without the help of drugs, but I told her I'm not a drug dealer." He sneered at her in disgust. "Apparently, Rich wasn't above sinking that low. He found her a new supplier before going to jail for trying to kill you."

"I knew I shouldn't have trusted him with that task," Olivia said and began to pace, speaking as if we weren't there. "He was too weak, just like my Tony. I loved that man so much, but he was bad at managing money and had a gambling problem of his own. I was not going to let him ruin our family name. He would never drug his precious horses or kill anyone. He had no idea I'd resurrected a little family history, or that I was behind any of this." She turned and locked eyes with mine, hers looking wild and crazy. "After your reading, he figured it out and threatened to come clean. I had no choice but to kill him as well." She paused, her eyes going from sad to filled with hatred. "That one hurt a little bit. Tony really was the love of my life, so it's going to be a pleasure killing you."

Olivia pointed her gun at my stomach, and suddenly, I was transported back in time seventy-five years ago to Salvatore Ventura and Detective Fellini facing off. I picked up where I'd left off with my reading for Antonio, feeling and seeing everything he had. A loud bang sounded and I dropped to my knees and covered my stomach, but I didn't feel pain. How was that possible? I opened my eyes slowly and saw my mother standing over Olivia with a two by four in her hand.

Olivia lay on the ground, clutching her bleeding head with her hands. "Thank goodness you're here, Vivian. Your daughter tried to attack me." She let out a sob.

"Drop the act, Olivia," my mother ordered, still holding the wood as she stepped over the woman to rush to my side. "My daughter did no such thing. Unlike you, I have an honest family I can be proud of."

Olivia's hand inched toward the gun.

"Don't make me hit you again, Mrs. Ventura," my mother said in her best lawyer voice that gave me shivers. "Thanks for the strength class. You taught me well." My mother's gaze never left Olivia's face as she asked, "Are you okay, Sunny?"

I sat up and inspected myself. "I'm okay, and thanks, Mom. I love you."

"Love you too, darling." Her face transformed into a fierce Mimi bear. "If she hurt my grandbaby, she's a dead woman."

"She's okay, too." I smiled, patting my stomach. I didn't know how I knew that, but some strange bond passed between the three of us, linking us together for life. "You got Olivia under control?"

"Oh, she's not going anywhere. Make yourself useful, Mark, and tie her up." My mom nodded toward Olivia as she stepped forward to kick the weapon far out of reach, still holding the wood like a batter ready to swing. Tough lawyer had morphed into protective mother and a Mimi you didn't want to mess with.

Mark gladly did as he was told. "I don't care what happens to me anymore. I'm telling the police everything I know. You didn't deserve Antonio Ventura for a husband. I can't believe you killed your own husband. I hope you rot in jail forever."

Olivia looked away, holding her head slightly less high.

"I'll call Mitch," I said and proceeded to call in what had just happened. I hung up and Morty appeared, jumping into my lap once more. He was calmer than he had been in months as he looked deep into my eyes.

And suddenly I knew the truth.

EPILOGUE

Seven months later, I pulled up to Divine Inspiration in my brand-new white minivan with orange, yellow, and pink flowers painted on the sides. A surprise gift from my husband after the birth of our daughter. He climbed out of the passenger seat and grabbed the car seat from the back. Heading inside, we took our seats in the living room.

My mother and father were hosting a birthday party for Great-Grandma Tootsie's one hundredth birthday. Harry, Fiona, Granny Gert and Captain Walker were helping out as usual. I had even successfully baked a dish for the meal. None of us let Toots lift a finger. Mitch held little Martina, named after his sister. He had barely put her down since her birth a couple weeks ago. Martina looked just like her daddy with dark hair and stormy gray eyes and exactly the same temperament.

I couldn't love her more.

"Just wait until your son arrives," Granny Gert said. "That one will be quite the character, just like his mama, and his gift will be strong. Trust me, I know these things." She winked. Helga had been helping her to hone her skills, and Granny was an A plus student.

Mitch's face paled.

"Don't worry, it won't happen for another year yet."

Now *my* face paled.

"I still can't believe we have a baby girl, too," Zoe said.

The moment Sean had been cleared as a murder suspect, they'd surprised everyone and eloped. Not wasting any time making up for all the tension that had been between them, they'd conceived a honeymoon baby as well. When Zoe went into pre-mature labor, I realized that was the two babies I kept seeing in my visions. They weren't twins at all, but they were going to be as close as sisters.

"Don't worry, these two little terrors will show them the ropes," Jo said as her twins were walking now and into everything.

"I wouldn't exactly call them little, babe," Cole said.

"And whose fault is that, Sasquatch?" Jo shoved him after one twin while she sprinted in the other direction, catching the rascal just before he put a cat toy in his mouth.

Just then the doorbell rang.

My parents had invited Toot's remaining family to join us.

Great-Grandma Tootsie opened the door in excited anticipation of seeing her loved ones, saying it had been far too long. Except, a man with snow white hair and a plaid bowtie stood there with a bouquet of flowers.

"Detective Fellini?" Toots asked, staring at him in disbelief.

He swept his hat off his head. "These are for you,

Toots." He handed her the flowers. "I'd say they are long overdue."

"Is this your fella from long ago?" Granny Gert asked, looping her arm through Captain Walker's arm. He'd retired after Audra Grimshaw's murder case was closed.

"This sure is. I can't believe you're here," Toots said with tears in her eyes.

"May I come in?" The man had tears of his own glistening. "It's kind of a long story."

She stepped back and he came inside, walking around the room and shaking everyone's hands until he came to me. I stood up and he gave me a big hug, then leaned back and said, "Hi Sunny, it's wonderful to officially meet you. My name is Mortimer Fellini, but you can call me Morty."

We all sat down to listen to quite the tale.

While detective Fellini was dying he saw a white barn cat, who he thought had come to comfort him in his final hours. As he made his vow to not rest until he got justice over the Ventura family and all they had done, and to someday be reunited with his lady love, something strange happened with the cat...

"That cat lay on my chest while I took my last breath. Our eyes met, and I felt a shift in my body. I thought I must have been dying for sure because I heard a voice tell me not to worry, my work wasn't over. The next thing I knew I was seeing my former body from the eyes and body of the white cat."

The trio, along with my mother, gasped from where they were perched on the edge of their seats. Toots held one hand over her heart and her beautiful eyes were filled with a love I hoped I would always have with my handsome detective. Mortimer went on to say that once he met me and Granny Gert, he felt connected to us because we were psychic, but he never stopped seeking justice. Once Great-Grandma Tootsie came to stay at the inn, he couldn't help but want to be with her. He was close to finding justice and longed to be with the woman who stole his heart all those years ago.

"I had a job to finish before I could be with my Tootsie. I knew Sunny was in good hands with her detective, which gave me the freedom to put the final clues together while also spending more time with Toots." He winked in her direction and her wrinkled cheeks turned all rosy before she blew him a kiss. "The cat and I had a deal. Now that justice was served, he was free to be a cat again. Through some miracle over all these years, my body had been preserved at some mysterious location, and I was suddenly occupying it once more. I'd never crossed over to rest in peace."

Speaking of cats, Morty entered the room walking much slower than normal. His fur was still white, but no longer glowed, and a gray strand stood out on the top of his head. He leaned down and ate a piece of food off the floor for the first time ever, then jumped in my lap and purred.

Mortimer kneeled in front of Great-Grandma Tootsie and held both of her hands. "You knew I'd come back, didn't you?" To which Toots nodded. "I've missed you enough. There was no way I'd miss the love of my life's one hundredth birthday. And whatever time I have left in his century old body, I'm spending with you... By now we were all in tears, and our strapping men were trying hard to disguise theirs.

I'd moved to Divinity to escape my family and be independent, never expecting that this small town would give me so much. I looked around the room and felt blessed. As I cuddled Morty thinking of how far I'd come, how much I'd grown and how much more there was to do, I couldn't imagine not being surrounded by all of these people I loved. My handsome husband must have caught me grinning because he leaned over and kissed my cheek.

"Do I even want to know what's going on in that head of yours, Tink?" he whispered next to my ear, a slight grin appearing when I wagged my brows.

"Oh, you most certainly do, detective. I think Martina needs a nap."

And that's another story...

ABOUT THE AUTHOR

Kari Lee Townsend is a National Bestselling Author of mysteries & a tween superhero series. She also writes romance and women's fiction as Kari Lee Harmon. With a background in English education, she's now a full-time writer, wife to her own superhero, mom of 3 sons, 1 darling diva, 1 daughter-in-law & 2 lovable fur babies. These days you'll find her walking her dogs or hard at work on her next story, living a blessed life.

OTHER BOOKS BY KARI LEE HARMON

WRITING AS KARI LEE TOWNSEND

A SUNNY MEADOWS MYSTERY

Tempest in the Tea Leaves

Corpse in the Crystal Ball

Trouble in the Tarot

Shenanigans in the Shadows

Perish in the Palm

Hazard in the Horoscope

OTHER MYSTERIES

Peril for Your Thoughts

Kicking the Habit

DIGITAL DIVA SERIES

Talk to the Hand

Rise of the Phenoteens

WRITING AS KARI LEE HARMON

Destiny Wears Spurs

Spurred by Fate

Project Produce

Love Lessons

COMFORT CLUB SERIES

Sleeping in the Middle